Of Gods, Guitars and Grafters

Also by Colin Rogers and published by Ginninderra Press
From the Mallee

Colin Rogers

Of Gods, Guitars and Grafters

Of Gods, Guitars and Grafters
ISBN 978 1 76041 980 6
Copyright © Colin Rogers 2020

First published 2020 by
GINNINDERRA PRESS
PO Box 3461 Port Adelaide 5015
www.ginninderrapress.com.au

Contents

Don't Mess With the Gods

They called it the Bilges because someone had likened it to the gloomy and rat-infested lowest part of a boat. In fact it was bright, and spacious, and no one had ever seen a rat – if you didn't count Daryll. But 'Packaging and Labelling' was in the sub-basement of Stanton's Family Department Store so everyone called it the Bilges.

Anne reached for the next article: a set of six ugly shot glasses. Who buys this crap? Probably going to be a gift for some poor bugger who already had a set of useless shot glasses. Nobody would buy this sort of rubbish for themselves. So, tissue wrap each glass and stuff them in a '6-com-sml-carton', run a strip of the awkward two-inch tape right around the lot, check the order number and shove it along the counter to where Wendy Wombat printed the address label with a 6B pencil.

She wasn't really called Wendy Wombat. She was actually Wendy Coleman – like in the Coleman Medal that Ron Evans had won for kicking the most goals for Essendon. Not that Wendy could kick goals – she'd have trouble getting off her own broad backside. And she had a bit of a moustache and a bit of a beard and hairy arms. So she was, in Anne's mind, Wendy Wombat.

Actually, truth be known, Anne had got along with Wendy in the two weeks that she'd been working in the Bilges and she never mentioned her Wombat tag to anyone else. Besides, wombats were dumpy and inoffensive – kind-of Dooby-Do animals. That suited Wendy down to the ground, so to speak.

Basically she was really shy because of her – not to put too fine a point on it – appearance. She never ventured up to the staff tea room but preferred to use her own electric kettle down in the Bilges. Anne had twice brought her lunch back to sit and chat with the Wombat. It occurred to her that the Burrow might be a better euphemism.

The two little birds on the opposite side of the wrapping bench were Tweety-one and Tweety-two. Like in the Tweety-bird and Sylvester cartoons. They were almost identical Chinese girls. Maybe about mid-twenties, maybe mid-forties. Hard to tell; some of those lucky Chinese women never seemed to age. They were really nice girls but stuck to themselves and mostly just chirruped away in Cantonese so Anne struggled to keep up with what they were talking about. She'd made an effort to pick up a bit of Cantonese – always been pretty good with languages and accents.

Through their pigeon-Cantonese-English, she'd learned that the Tweeties were planning to open a Chinese restaurant when they'd saved enough. They already had a name for it: *Hǎo jiā,* which apparently meant Good Home.

The service lift gave a ping and Daryll pushed in another trolley-load of crap-to-wrap. That's what Daryll did: bringing orders down to Packaging and Labelling and then taking them up to ground floor to Dispatch and Mailing. He always quipped, 'Down to PALs, up to DAMs.' It didn't make any sense to anyone but his stupid self.

Daryll was a sleaze-jerk and he smelt bad but he thought that he was God's gift. He'd tried it on with the Tweeties and he'd tried it on with Anne. He'd left Wendy Wombat alone. Probably scared that she'd take him up on it if he tried. Jeeze, Daryll and Wombat – that's the sort of image that would put you off your food.

The Tweeties pretend not to understand Daryll. They just turn to each other and giggle in Cantonese, which is a really effective put-down. No bloke likes having attractive women giggling about him. Especially when he doesn't know what they're giggling about.

Anne had to be a bit more circumspect, because Daryll looked like the type of bloke that could get nasty if you just told him to 'F-off'. She started calling him Terrordaryll but he got it all wrong in his stupid head and thought that the 'Terror' was a bit of a lopsided compliment.

What she'd meant was that Terrordaryll sounded like Pterodactyl – a flying reptile.

So, when he slithered up too closely, she'd waft her hand in front of her nose and say something like, 'Jeeze, Daryll. What've you got in the trolley? It really pongs.' Or she'd look across at the Tweeties and chirp, '*Xiǎoxīn xīyì*', which always had them in fits of giggling.

Daryll had never figured out what she said, so he couldn't tell whether it was insulting or not. It was: a *Xīyì* is a lizard. Sometimes she'd slip in a *Chánchú* – a toad – which also brought on the giggles.

'G'day, Anne,' he leered as he slowly unloaded his trolley onto the wrapping bench. 'You're looking particularly delicious this morning.'

She offered an enormous sniff and affected her best nasal voice. 'Jeeze, Daryll. I don't feel delicious. Got a bloody runny nose and a shit-house headache. Reckon it's the bloody flu.'

He backed off. Nothing like a runny nose to put a bloke off his game. 'Oh, that's…that's not good. Nah, not good.'

Anne looked across at the inquisitive Tweeties, winked and nasalled, '*Huài bìng*. Bad disease.'

They fell about giggling while Daryll slithered his trolley back into the service lift and pressed 'Up'.

*

They called it the Gods, which was wrong. Someone, trying to sound like a sophisticated wit, had given the sobriquet to the hallowed Stanton Boardroom on the fifth floor. The Gods, which Anne, seven levels below could tell you, was traditionally the highest part of a theatre's auditorium – furthest from the stage and where the cheapest seats were. It was called the Gods because you could look down on everyone and also because you were closest to the mythological themes painted on the ceilings.

None of this was of interest to Nyles Botham nor Alexander Stanton, who each sat, flanked by their best lawyer and their head accountant, as they studied each other across the enormous polished black-wood conference table.

Truth be known, Alexander Stanton, as the co-owner and major shareholder in Stanton Family Enterprises, rather liked the Gods. He was aware that the phrase was wrongly applied but it suited his wry sense of lopsided self-awareness to be considered as a Bacchus or a Dionysus.

Nyles Botham, on the other hand, couldn't care less about Bacchus or Dionysus. His gods, had he even a smattering of classical education, would probably be Plutus or Bonus Eventus. He was here to buy out the stuffy old fart and then to close down his outdated department store. Not that he'd ever call Stanton a stuffy old fart in public. Well, not until the deal went through. For now, he'd pander to the stuffy old fart's ego.

Stanton's was obviously failing because Alexander hadn't kept up with the current trends in retailing like his competitors' flashy television advertising and promotions. He hadn't noticed that eighty-four per cent of the customers who walked through his doors were over sixty nor that two of his competitors had merged and turned half of their premises into a multilevel car park. He hadn't even noticed that his best lawyer and his head accountant had been lining their own nests against the day when someone like Slimy Nyles came knocking.

Nyles had all the facts and figures at his fingertips thanks to his lawyer on one side and accountant on the other. Not that he'd ever been known to thank them for only doing their overpaid jobs. Nyles's task, that part of all negotiations that he loved best, was now to gently make Alexander Stanton cognisant of the undeniable, but terribly terribly sad fact that Stanton Family Enterprises was going down the tubes and that his best option was to sell out to Botham Investments.

He'd crossed paths with Stanton and the Tonkin Twins years ago but doubted that they'd remember him. The one on Stanton's left, with the beard, was Alf, the lawyer. The one on his right with the bristly crew-cut was Andy, the accountant. They'd all played cricket for the university's first eleven – what, forty-odd years ago? They'd lost the grand final to Nyles's team, Mortonvale, when he'd been a demon six-teen-year-old pace bowler and a safe pair of hands in the slips. He remembered that it had been a very narrow victory and not without some controversy and ill-feeling. Too bad – he had the trophy photograph hanging in his office and these clowns had bugger all.

Since those glory days, he'd become, in his own eyes at least, a successful, some would say disreputable, wheeler-dealer with a nose for potential asset-stripping targets. Buy cheap, fire the workers, close the business, sell off everything and then redevelop the real estate on borrowed money and flog it off for a fat profit. He reckoned that Stanton's Family Department Store was ripe for just such a killing if approached carefully. This sort of negotiation had to be handled gently because Stanton was third-generation and had third-generation sentiments about tradition, and loyalty, and principles.

*

If there was one good thing about this job, and God knows there weren't many, it was that it gave a girl plenty of thinking time. In the two weeks that she'd been in the Bilges, Anne had mastered the art of switching her hands to autopilot while they wrapped up the packages. This left her brain free to get stuck into some thinking.

And Anne had plenty of thinking to do. She could think loving thoughts about her three-year-old daughter Lucy – Lucinda. She could think loathsome thoughts about Mick the Mongrel husband who, last she'd heard, was behind bars somewhere up north.

She thought a lot about her parents, now in their sixties and as fit as trouts. Her dad worked from home as a structural engineer and lectured at the university two days a week. He'd converted one of the many bedrooms in their rambling old house into a studio with all the latest gizmos like full-keyboard electric calculators and electric pencil sharpeners. The latest in map drawers and filing cabinets in fashion colours shared space with two enormous drafting tables.

Her mum, Patricia, had come from a rather well-to-do family and, as a consequence, was something of a socialite, albeit something of a reluctant socialite. She'd inherited not only a healthy bank balance but also a circle of her parents' socialite friends' siblings. In marrying Oliver, she'd chosen from outside the circle and in falling pregnant with Anne she'd further distanced herself from them. Patricia felt no regrets about that but it had left a bit of a hole in her life.

Anne and Lucy had filled that hole when they moved back in with Patricia and Oliver after Mick the Mongrel had shot through. Sharing the house with her parents had been a bit awkward at first but it was working out pretty well now that they'd fitted out two of the back bedrooms like a discreet granny flat. They loved Lucy and spoilt her and the house was only ten convenient minutes by train to Stanton's.

Mostly what she thought about was the Ironmongers Theatre – a local dramatic society that had made its home in what used to be a hardware and paint shop. In a weird way, it was because of the Ironmonger's that she was currently crap-wrapping in the Bilges.

She'd not enjoyed uni. Well, the university itself was OK but the business management course that she'd pursued as a sort of obligation to the family's retail dynasty just didn't suit her. The only really enjoyable aspect of her three years was the university's repertory and comedy theatre. She'd signed up during orientation week and never regretted it because it introduced her to some of the most creative and funny people on campus.

It hadn't taken long to gain a bit of a reputation for her ability to mimic, in both voice and mannerisms, an impressive list of politicians, celebrities, sporting heroes and academics. No one was immune from her comedic satirical impersonations.

Ultimately, her theatrical pursuits started to overwhelm her academic results and she barely scraped through to gain a diploma that she was never likely to make use of.

*

'Thank you again for seeing us, Mr Stanton…'

'Please, it's Alexander.'

'Oh, well, thanks again for seeing us…Alexander.'

'You're welcome. Would you like a tea or coffee?'

'No, we're fine, thanks.'

'Right. Then perhaps you'd better confirm why you're all here.' Alexander Stanton made a small open-hand gesture to indicate all three men sitting opposite. 'Although…' and here he indicated the men sitting on either side of him, '…I'm pretty sure that we already know. You're going to make me an offer that I can't refuse, aren't you?'

Nyles Botham flashed a lizard's smile. All that was missing was the forked tongue. 'I doubt that it'll come to that, Mist– er…Alex…'

'Alexander.'

'Sorry…Alexander. I doubt that it'll come to that. All I'm hoping to do this morning is suggest a few possibilities.'

'A few possibilities about an offer I can't refuse,' repeated Stanton. 'Well, no point beating about the shrubbery, Mr Botham…'

'Please, it's Nyles.'

'No point beating about the shrubbery…Mr Botham. Make your pitch.' Alexander Stanton made a point of pulling back the sleeve of his crispy-white business shirt and studying an ancient and chunky wristwatch. 'I've a luncheon meeting with someone important.'

'Not bad,' thought Alf Tonkin, sitting to his left. 'Two little poison darts in one phrase.'

'Right, good.' Different smile; same lizard. 'You're no doubt aware that, during these past two months, Botham Investments has been purchasing Stanton Enterprises shares –'

'Eight per cent,' interjected Stanton and looked to his accountant for confirmation.

Andy Tonkin nodded agreement. 'Two point seven per cent of the total. Yes, we know. And at nearly thirty-two per cent above the market price.' And before Nyles could lay down one of his trump cards, Andy added, 'I sold you a third of my shares.'

'Me too,' offered Stanton's lawyer, Alf Tonkin.

Nyles, somewhat taken aback by this revelation, frowned across the table at Stanton's men who, he'd just realised, were twins but aged enough to be no longer identical. Surely this was an act of disloyalty on their part. 'Er, did you…?'

Stanton gave his best patronising grin with head cocked to one side. 'They cleared it with me first, Mr Botham. In fact, it was me who suggested that they sell. Nothing wrong with chaps picking up a nice little profit when someone's prepared to pay over the odds.'

'No, right…I suppose…'

'Mr Botham, you've obviously done your research.' Stanton swept an arm to take in the boardroom. 'You know that when we floated our share issue to restructure this enterprise my sister and I each retained thirty-three per cent of Stanton Enterprises. The public issue, the maximum that you can get your hands on, is thirty-four per cent. So far you've got eight per cent of the public issue and looking for more. Why?'

Botham shrugged a faux-innocent shrug. 'I'm always on the lookout for sound investment prospects, Alexander…'

Stanton pushed a traffic policeman's 'Stop' hand towards Nyles. 'With all due respect, Mr Botham, that's a load of camel crap.'

'No, it's –'

'Mr Botham, your business, if you could call it that, is asset-stripping. You've got no interest in Stanton's other than its material worth. Please don't insult us by pretending otherwise.'

'No…no…Alexander. It's not like tha–'

Stanton rose. Somehow he looked taller – rigid. He leaned forward, arms stiff and with both hands planted on the table and flashed his best patronising smile again as his lawyer and his accountant also stood. 'I don't converse with liars, Mr Botham. I know you. Your intention is to gain control of my business and then dismantle it. You've done it before on a small scale. Close the business, fire the staff and sell off the assets. If you ever want another meeting, you can leave a note of apology with the receptionist and arrange a date.' He moved smoothly to the polished blackwood door and held it open for Nyles and his two-man entourage. 'Goodbye, Mr Botham.' He looked at his watch again. The meeting had taken four minutes.

*

Anne had no disillusions about the Ironmonger's. She knew that it was a tinpot operation with a shoestring budget and a cast that was mostly rank amateurs. But it was a terrific bunch of people who pitched in with everything from painting sets to serving coffees during interval. She'd even dragged her mum along to help out with the front-of-house and the costumes. Didn't have to drag her along any more: Mum was into it like a bee in a honeypot and just loved seeing her name on the program – Wardrobe: Patricia Neville.

Anne also suspected that Mum rather liked the little ego boost that came with being compared to her daughter. There wasn't any doubt that Anne took after her mother and, for that matter, Uncle Alex. The Stanton gene pool favoured tall, slim and stately. The comparison was emphasised by one or two silver-tongued blokes who offered such mildly flirtatious comments as 'Here come the Neville twins', or, 'Hey, gorgeous. Who's your younger sister?' The daughter would snort, the mother would blush and everyone would chuckle.

Anne had been the leading lady last month when they'd staged Everard's *Going to the heart of it*. The sets and props had been a real challenge but the black-humoured role of April Sunlight suited her down to the ground: beautiful, sardonic and cuttingly intelligent.

Mum had done a fabulous job with the costumes and the stage crew had devised some clever sets and lighting with projected images and silhouettes. Dad had loaned two of his sliding-tray projectors loaded with lots of fantastic images, so it had turned out to be a real family production.

But the real star had been the director, Angelina Dabinett.

A few people still remembered Angelina Dabinett from her onstage performances and even fewer from her infrequent appearances on television. She probably would have made the big time if she'd followed her agent's advice and offered herself to the advertisers and the news desks and the variety show producers. But Angelina was classically trained and classically scrupulous and, as a consequence, starred in a lot of low-budget stage dramas, a few upmarket Shakespearian productions and a handful of televised screenplays. These days she divided her time between directing at the Ironmongers and teaching performance techniques to private pupils. It didn't offer much in the way of financial rewards but two deceased husbands had left her with a house, a reasonable bank balance and her scruples intact.

Angelina Dabinett applied her own variation of Stanislavski's methods in that her pupils were firstly expected to master the fundamentals of stage performance before moving on to 'the art of experiencing', which was, basically, putting oneself into as many real-life roles as possible to experience and observe the daily nitty-gritty of most ordinary people's lives. As Angelina constantly reminded her pupils, 'You're cast as a gardener…there's no garden on stage…just props. You have to bring the garden onstage with you and convince the audience that you know how to pull a weed because you've actually pulled a hundred weeds.' Then she'd add with a twinkle, 'Not so easy if you're playing a psychopath or a corpse. Not what you'd call a walk-on-walk-off part!'

So it was that Anne worked in the Bilges, talking pidgin Cantonese, fending off Daryll and wrapping crap and all in the name of, the art of experiencing. Two weeks ago, she'd spent time behind the perfume counter and the week before that she'd joined the after-hours cleaners.

It had been easier for her than it had for Angelina's other six pupils. Having a family's department store at her disposal made it dead easy to slip into any number of different jobs – different experiences. The other pupils spent half of their time trying to convince various bosses and business owners that they were prepared to work for a week or two, without pay, just for the experience.

She probably could have wangled experiences in Stanton's for her fellow pupils but Angelina had expressly forbidden her. 'Don't do them any favours, darling,' she'd admonished. 'When you're all scratching each other's eyes out trying to land the same part no one's going to remember how nice you were. You've got the advantage – keep it.' Sometimes the wonderful Angelina could be a real hard case – a real hard-nosed lady canine.

*

It was a Wednesday when the old-fashioned wall phone suddenly gave a strident metallic jangle that had them all frozen. Daryll dropped a toaster and the Wombat dropped her pencil while Anne and the Tweeties stood rigid with strips of tape trailing from their fingertips. The jangling phone only ever jangled bad news like when an order was misplaced or broken.

Daryll answered after three nerve-racking cacophonies. 'Hello? Yes, she's here. I'll put her on. Anne…' he beckoned, and the guilt-laden relief in his voice was obvious. 'It's for you.'

Anne peeled the tape from her fingers and, taking the proffered handpiece, pushed Daryll aside and turned to face away from her intrigued workmates. 'Hello? Yes. All right.'

She hung up, grabbed her coat and handbag from the back of her chair. 'I've got to go,' she announced to the room in general and, when Daryll made to join her in the lift, she added a sotto-hissed, 'Piss off, Daryll.'

*

Her Uncle Alex met her in the corridor outside of his office. The short walk from the lift gave her time to judge his mood and, possibly, get an idea as to why she'd been summoned from the Bilges.

It didn't. He stood, as always, tall, straight-backed and looking somewhat aloof. Even as a little girl, that was how she always pictured him, although his wavy hair was now totally white and the wrinkles more delineated. She'd come to appreciate, particularly now that she was almost an actor, what a brilliant disguise his was. Not quite as extreme as the Doctor Jekyll and Mister Hyde transformation but the contrast between Uncle Alex the entertaining and generous family man, and Alexander Stanton the coldly pragmatic businessman was as good a theatre as you'd see anywhere.

'Hello, Anne,' he smiled warmly then laid a gentle hand on her shoulder and director her into his office. 'Let's go in here.'

Once inside, he directed her not to a chair at his desk but to a tapestry-covered settee placed to take in the city view from a tall window. He sat next to her and she could smell his *Pour Monsieur* cologne. Another little girl's memory.

'Anne, I won't beat around the shrubbery. I've just had a call from your father. Your mother's had a mild stroke.'

She said nothing. It took a second to comprehend what her uncle had said and then another two seconds to understand what it meant. Her mouth opened twice but the words didn't happen.

Alexander took the initiative. He took one of her hands in both of his and looked directly into her eyes. 'It's a mild stroke, sweetheart. Very mild. She's in hospital and she's conscious. A bit confused but conscious. Your father did an excellent job in getting her to the emergency ward… didn't wait for an ambulance…drove her there himself in record time.'

'But, how…?'

He squeezed her hand. 'That's as much as I know. Your father's at the hospital with her and I told him that I'd drive you in as soon as I could. My car's waiting downstairs. We should go.'

*

Alfred and Andrew Tonkin were the physical antithesis of their boss: shortish, balding and just a tad overweight. Alf, the older of the twins by eleven minutes, had a little less hair on his head than Andy but made up for it with a close-cropped beard and moustache surrounding the permanently smug family mouth.

Andy had opted for a no-fuss bristly crew-cut and clean-shaven dial so that, when seated behind a desk, it was not apparent that the two sixty-year-olds were twins. When they stood alongside one another, however, their twinship became more obvious because their statures and postures were mirror images and they both favoured snappy light grey suits.

Both were as sharp as green lemons and both had opted for professional careers. Alfred studied law, while Andy trained as an accountant. It had always been in the back of their minds that they'd combine their professions into some form of freelance consultancy. That had been many years ago and wasn't likely ever to happen because they'd fallen in with Alexander Stanton when all three had played for the university's first eleven. Alex's father had been a spectator when they'd lost the grand final by a whisker. Alex and Alf had contributed an opening stand of ninety-two and Andy had taken four for twenty-nine with his wicked wrist-spinners. Within three months, all three had joined Stanton's Family Department Store at the bottom rung of their respective ladders. Now all three regularly sat at the Gods polished blackwood table. Alexander as the Boss God and the twins as his wingmen.

Today, however, it was just the Tonkin Twins facing each other across the breadth of polished blackwood with the light from an overhead chandelier winking in a cut-crystal whisky decanter and matching glasses.

Alf took a decent swallow and reached for the decanter. 'So...any news about Alex's sister?'

'Nothing more than we already know,' replied his twin. 'Mild stroke...in hospital. He's taken his niece to see her.'

'Good lass, that Anne. Everyone says the same. You have to admire her tenacity. Flitting from one department to the next just to get experience.'

'Agreed. She could have walked into any number of decent jobs here if she'd wanted to. But no…she's dead set on becoming an actress.'

'My wife and I went along to the theatre to see her,' said Alf. 'What's it called? The Iron-something?'

'Ironmongers.'

'Yes, that's it. Anne played the lead in a silly thing called *Going to the heart* or some such. She really was quite good…carried the show. Rest of 'em weren't much.'

'Alex's sister – the one who's had the stroke – worked backstage. Sets and costumes and suchlike,' added Andy.

'Yes…saw that on the program. Right…' Small talk over, Alf addressed the business at hand. 'He's finally got back to you.'

Andy shuffled through a folder. He withdrew a small rectangle of card and slid it over the table. 'Hand-delivered by courier. All very cloak and dagger. Stupid really… I get a dozen letters every day by the normal post and I always open them myself. So a hand-delivered note is only going to draw the attention of my nosy parker secretary.'

'Please contact my office to arrange a meeting. N.B.,' read Alf. 'He's included his initials. How very indiscreet. Does he honestly believe that no one would connect N.B. with bloody Nyles Botham?'

'Well… ' Andy sipped his whisky. It was reasonable stuff – Famous Grouse. 'We know that knobhead-bloody-Botham has a penchant for the dramatic. That's why we agreed that you'd slip him your note at the last meeting. More clandestine. More sneaky. Let him think that we're the same as him…sly and devious back-stabbers.'

'Although he probably sees himself as extraordinarily clever and the rest of us as dumb bastards who can be manipulated to fit his ends.'

'Agreed. But, for now at least, that's the role we'll have to play if we're going to do business with the bastard.'

'More like going to do the business on the bastard.'

Andy smiled at his brother over the rim of his cut-crystal tumbler. 'Speaking of which, have you heard any more about Alexander's grand design?'

'No more than you. You've seen his brother-in-law's concept drawings. Ground floor and first-floor specialty shops and restaurants and suchlike.'

'And the rest of the building given over to luxury inner-city apartments?' completed Andy. 'Yep, seen all that. It all looks quite impressive and expensive.'

'Too expensive?' asked Alf of his accountant brother.

'Well, noooo. It'll be tight while the building's being redeveloped… no cash coming in. But it'll be worth four times what it's worth now when it's finished, so he'll have no problems getting finance. And the leases on the new specialty shops will bring in double what he's getting from the department store at present.'

'So…?'

'So it's a bloody brilliant plan.'

'And no wonder that knobhead Nyles wants to get his hands on the property.'

'Yair. Pity he's only about a year too late.'

*

Patricia Neville was sitting up in bed when her daughter and brother arrived. Her husband, Anne's father Oliver, was sitting in a straight-backed chair next to her bed and stood to shake his brother-in-law's hand while Anne threw herself at her mother in a smothering embrace.

'Oh, Mum,' she sobbed. 'I thought we'd lost you.'

From over her daughter's shoulder, Patricia looked quizzically at her husband and let out a pitiable and catlike meow. Obviously she'd been confused by the sudden noise and movement of the new arrivals and hadn't had time to process the event before she found herself near-smothered by Anne's embrace.

Oliver was quick to sum up his wife's confusion. He gently placed both hands on his daughter's shoulders and eased her out of the embrace. 'Come on, Anne,' he urged in a strong voice. 'Your mother's going to be all right.' In just a few words, he'd planted Anne and Mother in his wife's cognisance and thought that he'd caught a flicker of recognition.

'Here, Anne.' he continued more softly. 'Sit on the edge of your mother's bed.'

Anne took her mother's hand and gave it a squeeze.

'Anne,' whispered Patricia and nodded to herself as if in confirmation of who it was.

Choking on her tears, Anne managed, 'Uncle Alex brought me here, Mum…'

'Alex,' repeated her mother. It was a question, not a recognition.

'Alexander, dear,' added Oliver. He was about to add, 'your brother', but didn't need to because his wife's face lit up with recollection.

'Alexander,' she acknowledged. Then she smiled hugely and repeated, 'Anne and Alexander. Yes…'

*

They called it the Office because that was all it was and because none of them had bothered to contrive a light-hearted label like the Bilges or the Gods. These men were pragmatically cheerless – all business and all bastards.

Nyles Botham sat, every inch the oily-slick operator, behind his ultra-modern stainless steel and blonde-veneered desk. The Botham Investments lawyer Boris Bowich, and the head accountant Iain Feltus sat opposite him on ultra-modern and uncomfortable leather seats.

The much heavier, taller and balder Bowich favoured light grey suits, while the slighter built Feltus was never seen wearing anything other than charcoal-grey with pinstripes. Their only commonalities were to be found in their mutual deviousness and their sobriquets. Bowich, being totally bald, rejoiced in Boney; and Feltus, blessed with an unmanageable head of auburn hair, had been known since high school as Fuzzy.

'I have some interesting news,' announced Boney Bowich. 'Mrs Neville, Stanton's sister, has had a stroke.'

Both Nyles and Fuzzy Feltus looked at him.

'How did you come by that bit of info?' queried the accountant petulantly. It was in times like these, when kudos was in the offing, that the canny colleagues became cunning competitors. Their boss, who wasn't aware that his multiple bynames included Nifty and Knobhead, never acknowledged their efforts or achievements, so they'd drifted into the habit of attempting to upstage one another. They kept score by licking an index finger and drawing an imaginary 'one' in the air.

'From Alfred Tonkin…at Stanton's.' Boney Bowich licked his index finger and drew an imaginary 'one' in the air.

Fuzzy Feltus acknowledged the feeble victory with an eye roll.

Knobhead Nyles missed their gestures. 'Which one is he?' he asked. 'I can never figure out which one's which. Alf and Andy. Jeezus…sounds like a bloody Pommy comedy act.'

'Alfred is the lawyer,' informed Bowich. 'It was him that slipped me that note after our last meeting.'

'The note that suggested that we could do a bit of business with him and his crooked brother behind Stanton's back,' smirked Nyles. 'So much for employee loyalty. Give 'em a chance to make a few quid and most of 'em'll sell out.'

He pondered what he'd just said for a moment and then pointed his fountain pen at each of his own employees and growled, 'Don't either of you buggers ever think of going behind my back. I'm not as gullible as old Stanton and I know a few hard men who'd break your fingers for a bottle of Scotch.'

Bowich shook his head.

Feltus put up a 'stop' hand. 'No need for that, Mr Botham. You know that you've got our loyalty.' Another wet-fingered 'one'.

'Better had,' growled Nyles. 'So…Stanton's sister's had a stroke. Could be a stroke of luck for us, then. If we can strike some sort of a deal with her while she's not a hundred per cent…' He tailed off. 'Can you get some more information…like, how serious is the stroke, what hospital, how to get access to her without any of her family knowing… that sort of thing?'

'I'm fairly certain that the Tonkins will provide everything that we need to know,' suggested Bowitch. 'Best if I arrange to meet with Alfred and you…' he turned to Feltus, '…you arrange to talk with Albert?'

'What do we know already?' asked Nyles. 'About the family.'

'Stanton's sister…that had the stroke…is Patricia Neville.' Bowich consulted the folder balanced on his knee. 'Her husband's Oliver. He's a structural engineer and architect. Works from home. Highly regarded. Does some teaching at the university. One daughter – Stanton's niece – works at the store but not sure in what capacity. Involved in a dramatic society. Apparently pretty good.'

'What hospital?'

'Reeves Private. Very discreet…very expensive. I doubt we'd be able to get to her while she's a patient there.'

'What's her prognosis?'

'No idea. All Alf Tonkin could tell me was that she'd had a stroke. Nothing else.'

'OK,' Nyles repeated his pen-pointing. 'Get onto the Tonkins and organise meetings. Keep it really discreet…no restaurants or public places.' A pause for thought. 'In fact, that's what you should do…book private hotel dining rooms or suites with room service. Different venues. Wine and dine 'em. We're after information about how we can get her alone for a chat. Also whether they've any suggestions about which of Stanton's shareholders would be most open to an offer. Right?' When they both nodded, he added, 'Well, don't sit there like a pair of stunned mullets. Piss off and earn your pay.'

*

'Lobster frittata followed by duck à l'orange and a crème brûlée to finish,' listed Alf. 'In a private room at the Burnside. How about yourself?'

'The Westward. Discreet booths. I went for the truffles with marinated beef strips, the lobster thermidore and a tarte tatin,' answered Andy. 'Plus all of the appropriate wines. We ended up with brandies and coffee.'

'Of course,' nodded his twin sagely. 'Goes without saying. I assume that you followed the script? As did I.'

'To the letter,' nodded Andy. 'Patricia's stroke wasn't too severe and she'd be discharged tomorrow into home care with an agency nurse in attendance. Best time to visit would be this Wednesday when Oliver Neville is at the university and his daughter, Anne, would be working at the store. And, as we've arranged, the nurse will be occupied elsewhere so Nyles and Patricia won't be disturbed.'

'And how was the disreputable Boney Bowich?' queried Andy. 'Was he the perfect host?'

'Couldn't have been more accommodating. Lavish with his compliments and his food. Even offered to organise some late-night companionship if I so desired it. Which, I hasten to add, I declined.'

'Much the same from Fuzzy Feltus,' nodded Andy. 'Quite the smooth talker. I let him prise the information from me...made myself look guilty about it. He made a similar offer, which I also declined. Oh, he also hinted that Botham's might be upping their offer for Stanton shares but didn't provide any numbers. I said that we'd both seriously consider selling our remaining holdings to them.'

'Bowdich was particularly curious when I mentioned the rift between Alex and Patricia. About how they've been at loggerheads about the family business. How she'd been openly critical about the way he was screwing things up.'

'Yes, Feltus was the same. Seemed keen to know more, so I fed him the whole story. How she refused to attend meetings and complained about his management style. Oh, he also hinted that Botham's might be upping their offer for Stanton shares and I suggested that we'd both consider an offer.'

'Good. It makes sense that we wouldn't want to be holding on to them now that we know which way the wind is blowing."

*

'It's so pleasing to see you looking so well, Mrs Neville,' oiled Nyles. 'I was quite distressed to hear of your hospitalisation. I tried to contact Alexander personally.'

'Thank you, Mr…er…' Her words were slightly slurred and seemed to take longer than usual to put themselves together.

'Please, it's Nyles.'

'Of course…' She appeared to silently mouth his name before voicing it. '…Nyles. And please call me Patricia…Pat. I think…I think… best to keep things…less…less formal basis. Don't you?'

'Absolutely, Pat. Couldn't agree more.' He picked up the faux alligator-skin briefcase that had been sitting on the concrete paving.

They were sitting on metal chairs under the Nevilles' pergola, next to an impressive-looking barbecue and overlooking an expanse of groomed lawn studded with croquet hoops. The day was bright and breezy. Cool enough for a pale blue cardigan for her and a navy blue blazer for him. She also had a blanket over her knees and a headscarf, gloves and sunglasses.

Nyles had suggested that she might be more comfortable inside but she'd insisted on getting some fresh air.

Now he pulled a folder from the fake-gator and laid it on the ornate cast-aluminium table. Glancing around he asked, 'Er…I understand that you have a live-in nurse, Pat. Is she around the place?'

'Upstairs…bit of a lie-down,' answered Patricia uncertainly. 'I…I don't need her fussing.' She offered a bleak smile. 'You can…kee-keep an eye on me.'

'Fine, fine.' So, no one to eavesdrop or interrupt his spiel. 'Pat, I'm sorry to trouble you with this but I'm afraid I've got a bit of business to discuss with you if you feel up to it.'

'Oh? Well…yes. Some sort of business. Did…did Alexander send you?'

Nyles gave his best humble-chuckle. 'No, Pat. I had a meeting with Alex a week or two back but I'm here on my own behalf. Your brother hasn't raised any objections to me visiting you.' He opened the file while thinking, 'He can't object to what he doesn't know.'

'Just as well,' she mumbled, head down, addressing her gloved hands folded on the table top.

'Oh?' Nyles raised his groomed eyebrows in mock-unknowing surprise. 'I didn't know. Are things between yourself and your brother a bit…er…strained?' So, Bowich and Feltus had been on the money. There was trouble within the family. Excellent – trouble for them meant business for him.

'Strained…' She tested the word. 'Yes…strained. Haven't spoken a…civi-civil word for…for months. We…we communicate through lawyers.'

Nyles laid aside his folder and looked faux-genuinely concerned at Patricia. His twin reflections in her sunglasses confirmed his concern. 'Er…would it be presumptuous of me to ask why?'

She sighed. 'The business. The…the store.'

Wow. This was getting better and better. She's struggling with her speech but she knows what's going on. But play it gently, Nyles. You don't want the old bird going into a relapse.

Smiling one of his shaving-mirror-rehearsed ingratiating smiles, he offered, 'Pat, I've heard much the same on the street and I'm very sorry to hear it. I'm worried that it may be stressful for you to be talking about it. You are, after all, only a day or two out of hospital. Maybe I should ask the nurse to join us?'

'No, let her rest. I'm fine.' She rallied; sat up straighter in her seat. 'Just tell…tell me what you've come about. Then I'll lie down for a spell.'

'Well. I'm afraid it's about the running of the department store, Pat. We…my company and I…are in the business of resurrecting struggling enterprises and, to be perfectly honest, we have noticed a drop-off in your share prices that corresponds with rumours of a reduction in your retail activities.'

She nodded slowly.

He continued. 'It pains me to agree with you, Pat, but we also believe that your brother's management style could bring your company to its knees while other retail businesses seem to be thriving.'

Again the despairing sigh. 'Yes…yes…I thought as much.' For a long moment, she said nothing.

Nyles wondered if, behind those sunglasses, she'd nodded off. But then it became apparent to him that she'd been putting her thoughts in order. Rehearsing her words in her head.

'To be perfectly…honest. I'd…I'd sooner…nothing more to do with my brother. But…I've…we've…we need the income. Oliver's clever but got no head for…for finance. Half the time, he gives for…for free.'

Nyles shook his head in faux-sympathy. His reflections shook back at him. 'You know, Pat, if you sold your share of Stanton's and reinvested the money, you could still enjoy a reasonable income. My company could handle all of the investments for you. But the share price is falling all the time, Pat. You'd be advised to sell as soon as you can. Like I said, I could handle all of the negotiations for you…with no fee for service.'

'How long?'

This was almost too easy. Time for a bit more temptation. 'That depends on which way you want to go, Patricia. You could either sell your shares and reinvest or hang on until my company can get Stanton's back on its feet. My company sees Stanton's as struggling but with plenty of potential. My team of experts could have that place back in the black in…say, eighteen months.'

'Eighteen months?' She dropped her head, removed the sunglasses, screwed up her eyes and pinched the bridge of her nose. 'No, that's too long. I…I couldn't stand another eighteen months.'

'Possibly a little sooner if I took control immediately. The problem is, of course, your brother – Alexander. Unless my company can win control…become a majority shareholder…I can't do anything.'

She replaced her sunglasses before lifting her head. 'Majority shareholder? I…I don't follow you.'

'Cards on the table, Patricia.' Nyles opened both palms flat on the table in a nothing-to-hide-so-trust-me gesture. 'We've been quietly buying small parcels of Stanton shares at inflated prices. We've even bought some from your brother's trusted advisors. They've seen the writing on the wall. So far I've…we've…got about twelve per cent of the public issue. That's only about four per cent of the total but word is getting around that we're offering considerably more than market value. I'm confident that we'll get some more.'

'So…?' She queried. He wasn't sure that she was following any of this but he pressed on.

'So we need over fifty per cent of the total before we can start putting things in order. Trouble is, even if we could buy the entire public issue, we'd only have a third. Assuming that your brother won't part with any of his shares, it means that you and I need to come to some sort of arrangement.'

'What…arr-arrangement?'

'Patricia,' he oiled with deep concern. 'This is too much in one day. You're looking tired and I'm feeling guilty about discussing such serious matters when you're so recently out of hospital.'

'Yes, you're right.' Another deep sigh. 'I'm feeling tired.'

'Then perhaps we could meet again the day after tomorrow?'

'Yes.' She waved vaguely towards the house. 'Can you…you let yourself out…?'

*

'I suppose you two expected something a bit fancier for lunch,' commented Alexander Stanton as he reached for another roast beef and chutney sandwich. 'Now that you've had a taste of the high life.'

Alf Tonkin nodded and waved at the platter of mixed sandwiches sitting in the centre of the polished blackwood table. 'Well, I was rather hoping for a dollop of pâté de foie gras with my champagne-poached lobster but if chicken and mayo sandwiches are all that are on offer, then I suppose we'll just have to slum it.'

His twin brother took a sandwich and prised it open. 'No sign of white Stilton gold in here,' he sniffed. 'Just plain cheddar and mustard pickles. Very common.'

Stanton shook his regal head. 'My God. One slap-up feed with Botham's henchmen and you're both instant gourmets.'

Alf took a sip of tea. 'Hmm, this is just Earl Grey. I was hoping for Gyokuro.' He turned to his twin and put on his posh voice. 'I must say, Andrew, the standard of dining in the Gods isn't what it used to be.' Turning back to his boss, he enquired, in his normal voice, 'How's your sister getting on, Alex? Any more medical updates?'

'She had a visit from her doctor only an hour or so ago and Oliver phoned me. It sounds like encouraging news all round. She's very wary and uncertain of herself, which is, apparently, a typical reaction. A lot of stroke victims lose confidence in themselves. The live-in nurse that we've engaged has a lot of experience with stroke patients…lots of strategies. She's still having trouble with her speech and is very tired, so spends most of her days in bed or just relaxing.'

Andy put aside his plate. 'I had a call from Fuzzy Feltus this morning. No attempt at secrecy…no discretion. Called me his mate. Very excited about Botham's visit to your sister yesterday but didn't go so far as to explain what they talked about.'

'Just goes to prove what a slimy bastard that Nyles is,' frowned Alexander. 'What sort of a mongrel tries to do deals with a woman who's just had a stroke and barely out of hospital?'

It was a rhetorical question. No answer required. They each reached for another sandwich.

*

The weather was slightly improved; sunny and without the chill breeze. Nevertheless, she'd again favoured a knee blanket, gloves, headscarf and sunglasses.

Nyles was accompanied by his lawyer but didn't bother to introduce him by name. Instead he just stated, 'Patricia, this is my colleague,' as they took seats around the little patio table.

Mrs Neville didn't seem to notice Nyles's rudeness and acknowledged Bowich with no more than a small nod.

'I must say that you're looking much better, Pat,' began Nyles, despite the fact that he couldn't tell how she looked behind the sunglasses and scarf. 'How are you feeling?'

'A…a little better, thank you. Still get quite tired…forgetful. My nurse has me playing little games. Supposed to help. The doctor's prog-prognosis is for a good recovery. I've been lucky.'

That wasn't what he wanted to hear. 'Do you feel up to continuing our discussion of two days ago? I don't want to cause any undue stress or concerns. We could postpone until you're fully recovered.' Shouldn't have added that last bit…postponing is the last thing I want to do.

'No…no. Let's get on with it.'

'Fine, fine. Now…'

'My lawyer came this morning…"

Oh, bugger. Her lawyer. 'Very wise, Pat. Did he have any thoughts about how we might proceed?'

'Yes…yes.' She pulled a sheet of paper out from under her knee blanket and laid it on the table. Her gloved hands were trembling slightly as she tapped the paper. 'You read it.'

Nyles perused the single sheet and then passed it to Bowich, who quickly scanned it, nodded affirmation and passed it back.

Nyles continued, 'He's suggested that you should retain at least a small number of shares so that you can still have a voice in company affairs.' Damn it. 'Did he suggest how many shares, Pat?'

Bowich leaned forward and tapped the page with a finger. 'Oh, hang on. Here it is. Ten per cent.'

He read on to himself and then paraphrased what he'd read out loud. 'Which means that you could sell twenty-three per cent. However, that's on the understanding that I'd buy at the same price as I've been offering on the public issue. That would give you enough to invest and live on when combined with your husband's income.'

Damn again. He could strangle her lawyer, whoever he was.

'Sounds like your lawyer has come up with a sound plan, Patricia. So…nuts and bolts…I'll need to scrape together twenty-eight per cent of the public issue.'

'Christ,' he thought. 'So far I've got twelve per cent and it's cost me a bloody mint. If word gets out that I'm really on the hunt for Stanton shares, they'll go through the roof. I need to pin this woman down to a fixed price.'

'Patricia…Pat,' he lizard-smiled into the dual reflection of her sunglasses. 'As you know, the share prices are all over the place and, once I start serious buying of Stanton shares, it could start a run-on. If that happened, I just couldn't afford to buy the necessary shares.'

She smiled her wan smile. Any doubt that he had about her following the proposal was swept away with her next comment. 'You'd like a fixed-price offer?'

Damn. Where did that come from? 'Well, yes, that would be…'

She elegantly placed a small card on the decorative table. 'This is what my lawyer suggested.'

Nyles resisted the urge to snatch at the card. This wasn't going as he'd hoped. This woman…this stroke victim…this invalid female was starting to take the initiative.

Feigning casual indifference, he reached for the card. It wasn't as bad as he'd feared. He'd been expecting some outrageous amount. In fact, it was about fifteen per cent less than he'd been paying for the public issue shares. Nyles performed some quick mental gymnastics. He needed another sixteen per cent of the public issue plus Patricia's twenty-three per cent. Christ! Even at her lower price, it would still cost a bloody fortune. He'd need to find extra finance from somewhere. OK, one step at a time.

'Quite reasonable, Patricia. All the same, this will take some time to organise. I don't carry that sort of cash around with me.'

She offered a thin smile. 'I didn't think you would.' She pulled two identical documents out from under her knee blanket and handed one across the little table. 'My lawyer suggested this.'

Damn. That bloody lawyer again. He scanned the proposal and then, as before, passed it to Boney Bowich for his approval. Again, it wasn't as bad as it could be.

'So, this is essentially a guarantee that you'll sell seventy-six per cent of your shares. That's…' he turned to his lawyer with a raised eyebrow.

'Twenty-three per cent of the total,' offered Bowich.

'Right…so. Seventy-six per cent of your holdings at the agreed price to me only after I've secured twenty-eight per cent of the public issue.'

'I think that's what he said,' she hesitated, frowning; trying to recall something. 'I think he said that I had to sign that paper. You have to sign it too…I think that's what he said.'

Now there was a note of uncertainty back in her voice and Nyles sensed that she was losing focus. He felt a stab of unfamiliar emotion. Possibly sympathy? But it only lasted for a split-second before his normal state of indifference regained control.

She looked up. It was difficult to see her expression behind the sunglasses but her voice was weak and quavering as she asked, 'How…how does that sound…to you?'

More mental gymnastics. There was no possibility that he could raise enough money to buy all of the shares at one time. The banks wouldn't touch him, so he'd have to go, cap in hand, to the usurers…the sharks… and pay extortionist interest rates. But maybe…maybe…he could scrape together enough to secure the extra sixteen per cent of the public float. That would give him the necessary twenty-eight per cent. Then he could take those shares plus Patricia's guarantee to the banks and they'd be more likely to loan him enough to buy her shares. It would mean selling off all of his assets and probably remortgaging his house. Bugger; he'd only paid off the mortgage eight months ago with the profits from his last deal. Shit, the boat. Only had the Millkraft Flybridge cruiser for five months. Still owed a shitload on it. Ah, well, if needs must. In for a penny.

'Yes, Pat. You're correct. We both have to sign this guarantee and have it witnessed. Bowich here can witness it.'

He impatiently flicked a hand at Bowich to indicate that he should facilitate the signing. The lawyer, anticipating his boss's rudeness but saying nothing, withdrew a gold fountain pen from his pocket, unscrewed the cap and handed it across to Mrs Neville.

It was painful to watch the lady trying to hold the pen. The stroke had obviously affected her motor skills and her hand trembled noticeably as she managed a spidery and barely decipherable signature to both copies of the guarantee. Nyles added his own extravagant signature and Bowich witnessed the signings with his very pragmatically precise imprint.

That done, Nyles turned to Patricia. 'I'd need at least two weeks… maybe three…to organise everything. I can get my staff to immediately start securing the extra sixteen per cent of the public issue. Probably use a couple of shell companies to buy them so it doesn't look like I'm the only buyer.' He was only half addressing her and half thinking aloud. 'Yes, Pat…three weeks should do it. Can you hold out for three weeks?'

'That's…that's longer than I'd hoped for.' She shook her head wearily. 'I want it done before my…before Alexander hears. Just be as… as quick as you can, please.' She slumped back, seemingly exhausted.

'Have to give her a bit of credit,' thought Nyles, uncharacteristically. 'She's not done too bad for a stroke patient.' He rose and Bowich did likewise. They both gave a slight bow. 'Thank you, Patricia. I'll be in touch and keep you updated.'

She just nodded and then looked away.

*

'I've just come to pick up my stuff,' explained Anne to her curious ex-co-workers in the Bilges. 'My dad's at home looking after my mum and Lucy. I have to quit working here at least until Mum gets better.'

Well, it was kind-of a half-truth. Her mum was ill and her dad and her daughter were at home. But they'd be at home anyway – whether Mum was ill or not. She didn't mention that there was now a full-time nurse living in their mansion to look after Mum, nor that they had a full-time housekeeper who lived in the self-contained and nicely converted attic. Come to that, no one in the Bilges knew that Anne's uncle spent his working days upstairs with the Gods nor that he and her mother were co-owners of Stanton's Family Department Store.

There were chirps of sympathy from the Tweeties and a big, hairy hug from Wendy the Wombat, who added, 'Nearly morning coffee break, darling. Wanna stay for a cuppa?'

Anne checked the wall clock. Truth was, she really wasn't in any sort of a hurry. 'Yair. OK, Wendy. You whack on the kettle and I'll duck upstairs for a couple of finger buns.'

Once settled with coffee and buns and having told Darryl to 'Piss off', Wendy started plying Anne with questions. 'What's wrong with your mum? How long will you be away? Will you be coming back to work down here?'

It became immediately obvious that Wendy thought of Anne as a close and, sadly, only friend. She tried to steer their conversation away from any topic that might reveal her true status. 'The worst thing, Wendy, is that my mum can't help out at the Ironmongers now that she's crook. She was really enjoying it.'

'That's your acting group, right? Is your mum an actress?'

'Nah, not Mum. I've done a bit of acting there. I'm not very good but it's really good fun. Trouble is, we're doing a play called *Random Connections*...'

'By Peter Netherby, right?' interrupted Wendy.

Anne was stunned. 'Yair. That's right. How do you...?'

'I watch a lot of TV and I read a lot. Mostly magazines and stories about film and theatre. There was a feature story about Netherby in one of the mags. They might be making *Random Connections* into a mini-series.'

'I didn't know that.'

'Only a rumour.' She sipped her coffee. 'Anyway...what's the problem with your acting group?'

'Mum did most of the costumes for our last production and also helped out with the front-of-house...'

'What's front-of-house?'

'Mostly selling tickets, helping people find their seats, selling coffee and stuff at intermission. That sort of thing…'

'I could do that.'

Again, Anne was taken by surprise. 'What? Selling tickets?'

'Nah. Making the costumes.'

'You mean…like helping with…?'

'Nah. Like sewing and designing and pattern-making and stuff. I'm a fully qualified dressmaker, Anne. Got all the gear at home…sewing machine with all the flash attachments, overlocker, dummies…'

'Jeeze, Wendy. So why are you working down in this dump?" The moment she'd said it, Anne wished she hadn't.

The Wombat took a bite of finger bun and ruminated for a moment. 'Basically, Anne, because when you want to work in the rag trade, you're expected to start at the bottom. Doesn't matter how bloody good you are, you start in the sweat shop sewing up a thousand copies of someone else's designs. That's where I started, on the production line. But I was too slow and too careful. Didn't like to rush things. Other girls would sew up three dresses while I did one. I hated it.' Another bite and another sip. 'And also, Anne, because I'm a pudding. I'm fucking ugly. I'm…'

'No, Wendy… That's not…'

'Don't bother, Anne. You know it's true and I know it's true. I used to cop a lot of shit from the girls in the sweat shop.' She paused and shook her head at the memories.

Anne thought that she was on the verge of tears and was about to offer some sort of sympathetic cliché.

Then Wendy lifted her head, took a deep breath and continued. 'I know that I could get some hair removal treatments and lose a bit of weight. Hah…a bit? I could lose half a fucking ton and still look like a hippo. It's just a whole lot easier to work down here.' She finished the last two inches of finger bun in one bite – so much for weight loss. 'Actually, the money's a bit better here than it was in the sewing sweat-shop.'

There was no arguing with Wendy's self-evaluation, so Anne didn't insult her by trying. 'But you said you could make costumes. Did you mean…?'

'Listen, Anne. I come down here every day and talk to no one… you're the first one who's bothered in months. Then I go home, put on the telly or read a book and go to bed. Then I get up and come down here. It's a shit life, Anne. Like I said, I've got the dressmaking gear just sitting at home doing nothing. Just like me – doing nothing. You need someone to make your costumes? I'd like to give it a go.'

It was awkward but the tall and slender Anne left her seat and managed to bend down low enough to hug the Wombat while she remained seated. 'You're hired, Wendy.'

Then she gathered the coffee cups and plates and put them on a side bench next to Wendy's kettle. It wasn't a matter of tidying up – it was more a matter of hiding the fact that she was misting up.

Having dried her eyes with a tissue, Anne resumed her seat next to her new best friend. 'Wendy,' she began. 'There's a shitload of stuff that you don't know about me. You've been so upfront about yourself that I have to do the same. But you mustn't tell anyone else, OK?'

Wendy the Wombat nodded.

Anne continued. 'Firstly, Mr Stanton, the boss, the owner. Well… he's my…'

*

'Eighteen-point-five per cent,' said Feltus as he slid the summary across the tasteless blonde-wood desktop. 'A bit more than you needed but the last two sellers insisted on selling their entire block of shares.'

'So I only needed sixteen per cent but now I've got eighteen-point-five,' glared Nyles Botham. 'What sort of crappy negotiator are you, Feltus?'

His accountant shrugged. 'Like I said, we had to buy two largeish blocks to get over the line. Otherwise, we'd still be buying small lots and it would've taken forever.'

Nyles snorted as he read Feltus's summary of share transfers. 'And those last two bastards really screwed you for top money.'

Again the shrug. Feltus had busted a gut to get Botham's holdings up to the required twenty-eight per cent. Admittedly he'd paid over the top for the last two bundles, which were held by institutional investors. They'd probably conspired to bump up their offers. He'd have done the same in their shoes.

'We can sell off the excess once you've secured the Neville woman's third,' he suggested. 'Price will likely go up considerably once word gets out that you've got control of Stanton's.' He knew that Botham was, liquidity-speaking, on the bones of his bum. He'd remortgaged his big house, had to forfeit his boat for a fraction of what he'd paid off so far. All the stuff in storage, the residue of his last asset-stripping right down to the heap of second-hand office furniture had been auctioned off for much less than it'd been worth. He'd even downgraded his car; sold the Merc 190SL and bought an FC Holden, for heaven's sake!

He and Boney had enjoyed watching their boss jumping through hoops. Getting his claws into Stantons had become a fixation with him. It would be his biggest ever coup; put him one step further up the dung heap if he pulled it off.

They had no sense of loyalty to the bastard. He'd paid them well but treated them both like doormats, so watching him lose his composure and breaking out a nervous sweat gave them considerable entertainment. He'd made a few dumb decisions in his scramble for cash: his new home mortgage was at least a full per cent higher than it needed to be and he'd been absolutely dudded on the sale of his Merc. The auction of assets had been a disaster and he could have made money on his boat rather than just surrendering it.

They'd tried to offer advice in a half-hearted sort of way, tried to recommend better tactics, but he'd ignored them and just barged ahead. Sure, he'd raised the money and he had the shares but he was on the brink of bankruptcy. The whole pack of cards relied on the agreement with Patricia Neville. If, for example, Alexander Stanton challenged it on the grounds of her post-stroke competency, then Nyles was in knee-deep manure.

The phone rang. Nyles snatched at it. 'Yair?'

The lawyer nudged the accountant and gave a quick 'Let's get out of here' thumb jerk.

*

Boney Bowich accepted a coffee from Fuzzy Feltus and looked around his colleague's office, which was almost identically furnished as his own: the same bland blonde wood, glass and chrome rubbish which their boss had bought cheap at a bankruptcy fire sale. Feltus hadn't even bothered to replace the crappy oil painting, one of a job lot of twenty that their aesthetically bankrupt boss had also bought cheap. It was meant to represent a European autumnal forest scene but the nameless Taiwanese production line artist had got it terribly wrong – bamboo thickets weren't a common feature of European forests. Bowich had replaced his identical piece of visual insult with a much more subtle and subdued print of David Davies's *Summer Evening*. It confirmed his oft-stated opinion that lawyers were persons of high artistic judgement while accountants had their taste in their arses.

'I reckon that you and I will be looking for a new employer by the end of the week,' said the lawyer to the accountant as he reached for the artificial sweetener.

Feltus blew on his coffee; more a hiss than a blow. He was still smarting from Nyles's criticisms of his share purchases. 'If I last that long,' he grunted. 'I damn near handed in my resignation ten minutes ago. That bastard has no idea how difficult it was to purchase those last two parcels of shares. I swear the vendors were in cahoots.'

'I know. Knobhead was definitely out of order. Anyway, it wasn't only his short temper that I was referring to. Christ, the bastard's been treating both of us like dogs for years. If it wasn't for the salary and the perks, I would've been out of here long ago.'

'Best keep schtum about the perks, mate. What Knobnuts doesn't know can't hurt him. Incidentally,' he grinned across his desk, 'you'll notice a nice little deposit in your special account. Some of Nyles's share purchases included a brokerage fee, if you take my meaning.'

Bowich nodded. 'Thanks, mate. Appreciate it.' He and Feltus often clashed on business matters and they were always super-competitive when it came to collecting kudos. But when it came to perks, to skimming a little bit off the top without their boss noticing, then they worked in total accord, total harmony and, perhaps surprising for a pair of shysters, total honesty.

Feltus waved the lawyer's thanks aside. 'Don't mention it. So…you were pretty quick to get out of Nifty's office just now. What was it you wanted to talk about?'

'I wasn't joking about you and me looking for employment. I've got a feeling that there's something not quite right with the deal between Knobhead and the Neville woman.'

'What do you mean by not quite right? What have you noticed?'

'Nothing that I can put my finger on,' pondered Bowich. 'When he and I went to see Stanton's sister the other day, to get her signature on the deal, I just had a feeling that she wasn't how I thought she'd be. Y'know? Not how I thought a stroke victim would be.'

'Had a lot of experience with stroke victims, have you?'

The lawyer snorted. 'No, none. Like I said, it was just a feeling. But I also found it a bit odd that we didn't see anyone else. We know that Mrs Neville has a full-time nurse and a housekeeper but we never saw either of them. I mean, I know that Nyles's deal with her was meant to be confidential but you'd reckon that someone would have checked on her at some time.'

'Did Knobhead notice anything?'

'Nah. All he wanted was to get the share deal sorted out. Too busy doing his Mr Greasy-Smooth performance to notice that anything was unusual.'

'Do you reckon it could be challenged? Y'know, whether Stanton could challenge the deal on her competence?'

'Nah. She knew what she was doing. In fact, when I think back on it, I'd say that she was setting the pace…had all of her lawyer's documents ready…almost like she was playing our Knobhead like a violin.'

Bowich finished his coffee and stood. 'I've got a feeling in my gut that Nyles-bloody-Botham might have met his match in Alexander-bloody-Stanton.'

*

'Dad, this is Wendy.'

Oliver Neville rose from his seat at his wife's bedside and took Wendy's hand in both of his. 'Hello, Wendy. Lovely to meet you. Anne's spoken of you often.'

'Hello,' was all that the Wombat could manage. She was still coming to terms with her workmate's position, her status, in the Stanton hierarchy and now she'd been brought to this enormous family home. Who would have thought that the young woman wrapping crap in the Bilges yesterday would turn out to be the niece of the boss? It was exactly like so many of the B-grade movies that she'd scoffed at.

Anne's mum had obviously been dozing. The arrival of Anne and Wendy had roused her and she was struggling to shake off confusion and to figure out what was happening. 'Oliver?' she asked with a note of anxiety in her voice.

Her husband took her hand. 'It's OK, Pat. Look, Anne and Lucy have come to visit and she's brought her friend, Wendy.'

Anne leaned over the side of the bed to peck her mother's cheek and then help her to sit up in her bed while Oliver stuffed an extra pillow behind her and then lifted little Lucy up to sit at her grandmother's side.

Wendy took Patricia's hand. 'Hello, Mrs Neville. It's lovely to meet you.'

Anne now noticed that Wendy had somehow managed to rid herself of her moustache. Whether she'd just shaved it off or maybe found time

41

to have some cosmetic treatment, she'd have to ask later. Whatever she'd done, it'd made a difference. Sure, Wendy was still an overweight lump but now at least your attention wasn't drawn to her hairy top lip when she spoke. That, and the fact that she seemed happy…almost bubbly… changed not just her appearance but also her whole demeanour.

Oliver gave up his chair to his daughter and then dragged another across the room and indicated that Wendy should also sit while he stood at the foot of his wife's bed.

Patricia seemed to have overcome her uncertainties and was now enjoying her visitors. 'What do you do, Wendy?' she chirped.

'I work in the packaging department at Stanton's. With Anne.'

'Packaging?' The doubt returned. 'But I thought that Anne…?'

'Part of my acting training, Mum.' Anne tried to explain but it obviously not making any sense to her mother, so she changed her tack and gave her friend a wink. 'I was helping Wendy when she got snowed under.'

'Oh, that's…nice.' She looked to her husband and pointed to her mouth. It was obviously a recognised signal, because Oliver moved to her side, held up a water glass and helped her negotiate the paper drinking straw. Lucy watched the process in wide-eyed fascination. She'd never seen grown-ups drinking through a straw.

After several short sips, Patricia nodded and he removed the straw and glass. 'Thank you, dear,' she whispered. Turning to her daughter, she began, 'Anne…' But then she hesitated and frowned. 'There was something… Oh bugger!' She slammed both fists down into the coverlet in frustration. 'I keep…' Her words ended in a long, drawn-out sob followed by an intake of breath. 'I get so…so…'

'Frustrated, Mum?' offered Anne.

'Frustrated. So…frustrated. In my head but can't…can't…words.'

'That's what the doctor said, dear.' Her husband squeezed her shoulder. 'It happens to everyone who's had a stroke. You know what you want to say but the words won't come out.' He looked across the bed to the two girls. 'He assured us that it'd soon be…'

'The costumes…' His wife cut across him triumphantly. 'The costumes, Anne. What about the costumes?' It was a question but it was also a little victory – a thought that had become a sentence. The relief on Patricia's face was a joy to behold.

'Don't worry about the costumes, Mum. Wendy's said that she'll help with them until you're ready to get back into it.'

'I hope you don't mind, Mrs Neville,' offered Wendy. 'Anne told me that you might need to rest up for a while, so I volunteered. Only until you're better.'

Patricia leaned back against the pillows looked up to the ceiling and smiled. 'Good, good.'

Lucy slid carefully off the bed and trotted around to the other side to climb onto her mother's lap. Anne gave her daughter a gentle squeeze and spoke over her head. 'Do you remember, Mum? We're doing a play called *Random Connections*? Starts in four weeks, so…'

'*Random Connections*,' repeated her mother, and again. '*Random Connections*…yes.' Suddenly and with a look of huge concern on her face, she swivelled around to face her husband and cried, 'Oliver… you…you…'

'The sets and props, dear?' anticipated her husband. He took her hand. 'All under control, dear. We're going to use the projectors again and I've already got some of the images. The lads at the Ironmongers are already building the sets. They'd started it all before you had the stroke. It's all under control.'

'You'll be out of here in time to see the play, Mum. And by then you'll be well enough to start working on the next one. Wendy can be your apprentice.'

She may have heard Anne's assurances but probably not. She was asleep, still sitting up, gently snoring and with a contented smile on her face.

*

'He's got the sixteen per cent of the public issue.' Andy Tonkin passed several pages of figures to his brother sitting next to him and slid another set across the Blackwood to where Alexander would normally be sitting. 'Actually, a bit more than sixteen. Feltus had to pay a bit extra to get two institutional parcels.'

'How did you find out?' asked Alexander from where he stood at the tall, arched window. 'Through a mate in the stock exchange?'

'Nope. Fuzzy himself passed on the info. Another note delivered by courier. He's still under the impression that we're all conspirators… mates.'

The view from the Gods was always interesting, looking, as it did, along the length of Marriot Street and over most of the lower, nearby buildings. You could tell the time of day just by interpreting the bustle of commerce and the interaction of the pedestrians and traffic and trams. Stanton was always promising himself that, one day, he'd set up a camera to take a series of photos at different times of the day and in different weather conditions. Something like the series of Rouen Cathedral paintings that Monet had produced about seventy years before. Alexander didn't have any artistic skills whatsoever but he was a fairly dab hand with his Leica camera and had an extensive collection of extra lenses and filters and whatnot.

A dozen of his best framed photographs, some in colour, others in black and white, hung around the Gods and another fifty or so could be found in his office and along the corridors of the fifth floor. It was one of his few indulgences and vanities. Once this mucky business with Myles Botham was over, he'd definitely set up the tripod and start his Marriot Street series. This time for certain.

He turned back to the Tonkin twins sitting at the boardroom table. 'So, now he's got twenty-eight per cent of the public issue. If he puts that with the twenty-three per cent of my sister's shares, then he'll have the fifty-one that he needs to control Stanton's Family Department Store.

'But he has to raise the money to buy your sister's parcel,' reminded Andy. 'He's really been scratching for funds. He's remortgaged, sold his boat and his car. Fuzzy seems to be enjoying his boss's sticky situation. Not a good attitude for an accountant.'

'That's because Botham treats his staff like shit,' offered his brother and then turned to Anne, who sat silently at the end of the table. 'Oops…pardon the language, Anne.'

'Don't apologise, Alf. I've heard a lot worse.'

He nodded his thanks before turning to Andy. 'I mean, both Feltus and Bowich are bastards and crooks, so I don't have any sympathy for them but I can understand why they don't have any loyalty to Nyles.'

'Be that as it may,' interrupted Alexander as he resumed his seat at the blackwood table, 'we need to know how Botham intends to raise the cash to buy my sister's shares. He's got the signed letter of guarantee to sell, so where does he take it? Surely the idiot wouldn't go to any of the Shylocks?'

'I'm betting on the NatCo,' stated Andy. 'I was amazed that he found a bank that would remortgage his house so quickly. They must have figured that it's worth a lot more than they've allowed him. Probably rubbing their hands together in expectation of a foreclosure.'

'So you reckon that if NatCo were prepared to remortgage him, they'd also loan him enough to buy Patricia's shares?' asked Alf.

Andy smiled down at the file sitting on his lap. 'Providing that all of Knobhead's paperwork is up to scratch.' He looked up at his boss and his brother. 'And providing that NatCo doesn't discover the massive flaw in Knobhead's research.'

'The massive flaw that Boney and Fuzzy haven't discovered,' reinforced Alf.

Alexander Stanton turned back to the view and addressed the window. 'Are you absolutely certain that Bowich and Feltus haven't found the flaw in Botham's plan? I mean, could it be that they just haven't told him that they're just sitting back and watching him sink himself?'

'Possibly,' nodded Alf. 'It's the sort of thing those two mongrels might do if they realised that Knobhead was going under.'

Alexander checked his watch. 'Surely the brains trust at NatCo would pick up on such an obvious blunder. They're hardly likely to approve a loan without going through the procedures with a fine-toothed comb. Is there any way of checking? Do either of you have a contact at the bank?'

Andy scratched his crew-cut. 'I might do,' he pondered. 'Fellow plays in the same lawn bowls team. Not sure what department he's in but I could give him a buzz if you like.'

Alexander checked his watch. 'Fifteen minutes,' he announced. 'Yes, Andy. Give your mate a call and see if he's heard anything.'

*

Knobhead Nyles Botham was shown into the Gods exactly fifteen minutes later. That he wasn't accompanied by either his lawyer or his accountant was acknowledged with a surreptitiously quizzical eyebrow from Alexander to his niece and to his twin wingmen.

The handshakes were cursory before Stanton indicated that all should be seated. 'Let's not beat about the shrubbery, Mr Botham. You asked for this meeting. What do you want?'

Sitting at the end of the big blackwood table, Anne, ever the actress, would later remember the meeting as a perfect one-act play. The set was perfect: A classic boardroom with antagonists sat on either side of a huge table. The actors? Well, amateurs, certainly. The script? Probably best described as…as a work in progress. Alf would later describe Nyles's smug smile not as the over-used cliché 'cat that got the cream' but more like 'baby that's just done a relieving crap in his nappy and hasn't yet realised the long term consequences'.

It was Knobhead's most malevolent lizard smile with overtones of venomous sneer and malicious smirk. Interlocking his fingers in front of him, he leaned forward and let his slitted gaze fall upon each of them in turn until he focused directly on Alexander. 'I'm here to inform you that I'll be calling an extraordinary shareholders' meeting in exactly ten days from today.'

'Not bad,' thought Anne. 'Confident delivery with a heavy touch of malevolence and a good dose of shock value.'

'Oh?' queried Alexander in faux surprise.

The Tonkin twins tried to look aghast at each other but, as actors, they failed terribly. Anne struggled not to burst out laughing as she dropped her head and pretended to rummage through her tapestry shoulder bag. The twin's thespian offence went unnoticed by Nyles as Alexander Stanton continued.

'I realise that you've become a significant shareholder, Mr Botham, but I'm not sure that gives you the authority to call an extraordinary meeting. I'm not certain that I'll be available in ten days' time.'

He threw a questioning glance at Andy and Alf, who both went through a charade of checking their diaries before shaking their can't-be-there-either heads.

'Marginally better,' conceded Anne to herself. 'But certainly not Helpmann-winning performances.'

Nyles leaned back in his chair and his smile changed from insidious lizard to triumphant chimpanzee. 'It won't matter a damn whether you or your two clowns can't attend, Alex. Fact is, in ten days' time I'll be the majority shareholder of Stanton Enterprises.'

In near slow-motion, milking every gloating second for what it was worth, Nyles opened his faux-gator briefcase, removed a single sheet of paper and slid it across the table. 'You'll note your sister's signature at the bottom, Stanton. Signed in the presence of myself and my lawyer, who will testify that she was in a fit and coherent state when she signed it. We've also got copies of advice given by her own lawyer and which she handed to me just prior to signing this. Any claim that she wasn't fit to sign can and will be challenged.'

'Dear me…' began Alexander. 'But…'

'I also understand,' interrupted Nyles, 'that you and your sister weren't on speaking terms…that you only communicated through intermediaries and that she had expressed the desire to get out of the family business.'

Stanton went through the motions of studying the document. 'So, a guarantee that she'll sell you enough of her shares to give you a majority providing you'd already purchased twenty-eight per cent of the total. We've been keeping a watch on your purchases, Mr Botham. We know that you've achieved your goals. I can only assume that you'll be finalising the purchase of Patricia's shares within the next ten days.'

'You've got that right, Stanton. My accountant and lawyer will be knocking on your sister's door as we speak.'

'Except –'

'Nope, there're no excepts, Stanton. No ifs, no buts. I've covered all the bases. You're out and I'm in.'

'I was going to say, except the date, Mr Botham.'

A flicker of doubt crossed the Lizard Chimp's dial. 'What about the date, Stanton? It's right there…under our signatures. Witnessed and everything.'

'Yes, I can see that. It's just…' Alexander turned to his accountant. 'Mr Tonkin. Have you got my diary handy? I just want to check that date.'

More charades. Andy appearing to be searching for a diary that was, in fact, the only thing in his genuine-gator briefcase. Then he flipped endlessly through endless pages until he found the appropriate date which had been bookmarked anyway.

'Good use of props,' thought Anne to herself. 'Angelina Dabinett would probably give him a seven out of ten for this performance.'

'Ah…yes, Mr Stanton.' Sliding the thick diary across the blackwood table. 'Here it is.'

'Thank you. Ah, yes. I thought so. Seems to be a bit of a contradiction here, Mr Botham.'

Nyles snorted. 'Contradiction? Shouldn't think so, Stanton.' He pointed to the single-sheet document. 'All cut and dried.'

'It's just that my sister was confined to her bed on the date in question. In fact…' He flicked several pages to and fro. 'In fact, she was bed-bound for that whole week. Doctor's orders.'

'Might have been doctor's orders, Stanton. I can assure you that your sister, Patricia, sat with me on the patio of her house and signed that document with Boris Bowich, my lawyer, as witness.'

Alexander nodded slowly and in his most patronising, almost pitying, voice said, 'You see, Nyles, while you state that you were sitting on the patio with my sister, she was actually in bed. Oh, sorry, Nyles. I forgot to mention that the bed, Nyles, was in a private room in the Reeves Private Hospital.'

Botham made to interject but Alexander held up a restraining hand. 'And, while you claim that your lawyer was there as a witness, I can absolutely swear on a stack of Bibles that I was with Patricia for most of the day, the doctor visited her three times and the nurses were in and out of her room all day. There couldn't have been more than five minutes when she was left alone.' He nodded to Alf. 'Mr Tonkin, do you have those statements?'

The lawyer withdrew several papers from his own real-gator briefcase and placed them, like a card sharp laying down a full house, one by one on the blackwood table. 'These are duplicates. One here from Dr Hennessey, one from the Reeves' head nurse, this one from the housekeeper who visited her and brought in some personal items, one here from a Miss Wendy Coleman who, I understand, discussed costume designs. Here's one signed by yourself, Mr Stanton, and here are all the hospital admission records, copies of the prescriptions issued and the financial accounts and receipts. All accompanied by statuary declarations signed by a justice of the peace.'

Having laid out the winning hand, Alf grinned across the blackwood table at Knobhead. It was the ingenuous grin of a Hobbit. 'You also seem to be somewhat misinformed about Patricia Neville's lawyer, Mr Knob– er, Botham. It's me. I act on her behalf just as I do for Mr Stanton and the rest of the family. I certainly didn't offer Mrs Neville any advice on this matter.'

The ex-Lizard Chimp slammed the flat of his hand on the table. It must have hurt but, in Anne's eyes, it worked quite well – dramatically speaking.

'That's bullshit, you bastards,' he yelled. 'That's a pack of lies.' He jabbed at his single sheet, which now looked rather lost against the multiple sheets of Stanton's witness statements. 'Your sister signed that agreement…that, that guarantee.'

Alexander picked up the single sheet by one corner in much the same way as he'd pick up a soggy tissue. He pretended to study it. 'Well, someone signed it, Nyles. But it couldn't have been Patricia. As we've just proven, she was bed-bound in hospital and surrounded by friends and relatives and medical staff.'

As if on cue, Andy turned to his boss with an overacted, Anne would have called it melodramatic, look of concern on his face. 'How is your poor sister, Alexander?'

Stanton shook his head slowly and melodramatically. Once again, Anne had to drop her head, bite back a chuckle and check the contents of her shoulder bag. These blokes wouldn't get past the first auditions at the Ironmongers.

'She's much improved, thank you Mr Tonkin. These extra days in the Reeves Private Hospital have worked wonders. She'll be returning home tomorrow.'

'So that means…?' queried Andy in a truly horrendous example of leading dialogue.

This time, Anne had to bury her head in her bag to stem her mirth.

'It means that Mr Botham's accountant and lawyer can stand on her front veranda and knock on her door all day but they won't get an answer.'

Nyles was back on his feet and slapping the blackwood table once again. 'This is bullshit,' he repeated. 'You've just stuck her back in hospital so that she can't sign over her shares. You've…you've kidnapped her. Everyone knows that you and her've been fighting for years. You've…you've abducted her. That's a criminal offence, that is.' He leaned across the table and jabbed a finger, pistol fashion, at Stanton's chest. His words were accompanied by flecks of white spittle. 'The cops, Stanton. I'm calling the cops. Abduction…they'll put you away for years…'

'Far too melodramatic,' observed Anne to herself. 'Not cool at all. Nobody reacts like that. Oh, hang on…he just did.'

Alexander stepped back from the table with a look of haughty distaste. 'Please don't spray your words, Nyles. It tarnishes the furniture polish.'

'Nice lines,' thought Anne. 'Cool and suave and well-delivered.'

Unaware of his niece's unspoken critique, Alexander continued. 'I don't know what you mean by my sister and me fighting. We've never had a cross word…always got along famously. As for kidnapping and abduction, well, I can always get another statement from Dr Hennessey and the nurse.' He turned to Alf. 'Mr Tonkin, would you organise for Dr. Hennessey to provide Mr Botham with a full diagnosis of Patricia's condition?'

Nyles, flushed and breathing hard, had slumped back into his seat.

This time, it was Alexander Stanton who leaned across the table and stabbed a pistol finger. His voice was a harsh hissing rumble. 'You've screwed up, Botham. You've been made to look a fool…no, I take that back…you've made *yourself* look like a fool. You're a greedy and dishonest little shit, Nyles. A small-time grubby little shit. I'm going to make sure that everyone in this town knows how you made a damned idiot of yourself, Nyles.'

'Not bad,' thought Anne. 'Somewhat overplayed and too many clichés. A bit too much like a B-grade American movie but, overall, not bad.'

Andy had moved to the door. He opened it and gestured to Nyles. 'This way, Mr Knob– er, Botham.'

Nyles stood and snatched at every piece of paper on the blackwood table. Stuffing them into his faux-gator briefcase, he snarled, 'I'll get you, you bastards.' Looking directly at his triumphant adversary, he screamed, 'You've not heard the last of me, Stanton.'

Anne grimaced. 'Oh, no…that's not even B-grade Hollywood. That's E-grade.' She opened her shoulder bag and began removing items. No one noticed.

Alexander offered an open-handed ushering gesture towards the door. 'I hope not, Nyles. Watching you screw yourself has been endlessly entertaining. Oh…' He paused and raised a single finger to the ceiling in a cricketing 'You're out' gesture. 'Something else for you to ponder, Nyles. Forty years ago, you claimed a catch in the University versus Mortonvale cricket grand final. You remember? You were in slips and you grassed a difficult chance off Mr Tonkin's bat. Everyone except the umpire knew that you'd put it down but you claimed it as a legitimate catch and Mr Tonkin was given out. We would have won that grand final, Nyles, if you hadn't cheated. I'm going to let the whole town know that you also cheat at cricket, Nyles. A lot of people will see that as the biggest of sins. Some people understand greed and skulduggery and some even condone it. But cheating on the cricket field? That's unfor-givable, Nyles. Now get out.'

The door closed and the Gods became a haven of silent satisfaction. The three men were on their feet grinning smugly at each other. They turned towards an 'Ahem' noise at the end of the big blackwood table, where they expected to see Anne. Instead, and decked out in gloves, headscarf and sunglasses, sat the figure that Knobhead Nyles knew as Patricia Neville.

'It's a good thing,' she said, 'a good thing that at least one of us is a passable actor.' She removed the sunglasses, then the headscarf and then she shook out her hair. 'You three were absolutely shocking.'

Cricket & Crotchets

Winter in Gunnery Bay can be a bit…well, to put it kindly, quiet.

Farmers do maintenance jobs while they watch the wheat grow in their paddocks and the wool grow on their sheep. The caravan park is empty, fishing is damn near impossible and the kids catch the school buses in the morning gloom, spend a gloomy day in the cold classrooms and then arrive home in the afternoon gloom. The only really interesting activity is the footy and that's only on Saturdays and they can be fairly gloomy if the Gunners go down.

Things really pick up in spring and early summer. Everyone becomes preoccupied with harvests, shearing and fishing and, if there haven't been too many gloomy Saturdays, a grand final needs to be won before the town's sportsmen swap their muddied jerseys for cricketing creams. Then there're holidays to contemplate, Christmas to celebrate and New Year's to negotiate.

You can't find a parking spot within a mile of the boat ramp, the caravan park is chockers and you can't move on the jetty for city dads removing fish hooks from their city kids' thumbs.

The Cannon Fodder Café, the Gunner's Arms Hotel, the Target Takeaway Restaurant and the Calibre Kiosk struggle to feed the invading hordes. And NatCom Rural (formerly Nationwide Community Bank) struggles to handle the deposits of small denominations that flow from those four artillery-themed but, particularly in the case of the Cannon Fodder Café, unfortunately named eateries.

Summer is when Gunnery Bay celebrates the Return of the Transients. As an event, it lacks the precision and romance of the Return of the Swallows to Mission San Juan Capistrano on 19 March of every year. Nor is it revered as a miracle. But then Mission San Juan Capistrano is in California, where folks declare their pizza to be a miracle if they find anything resembling a bearded face in the cheese topping.

The good folks of Gunnery Bay usually count on the arrival of seven or eight transients. Some are returning to positions held before the summer break, while others are filling positions vacated by previous transients. This second group will be new to Gunnery Bay and, more often than not, taking up their first placement since completing their training.

The locals don't call them transients to their faces. It's a bit unfriendly. A bit…expository. They greet them as our new teachers at the area school, or the new bank clerk at NatCom Rural (formerly the Nationwide Community Bank), or that new young chap in Faraday Farming (formerly Faraday's Stock & Station Agency).

The new blood is of interest for a number of reasons. Firstly; they all need accommodation. There is a thriving boarding house industry in Gunnery Bay which is controlled by a cartel of widows-who-own-large-and-largely-empty-houses. Most transients initially take advantage of the reasonable rates, reasonable meals and reasonable laundry offered by these enterprising ladies. After six months, most of them team up and rent an empty house where they can come and go as they please, eat rubbish food and entertain. The young, single blokes save up their laundry and take it home to Mum during the holidays.

The young and single lady transients are of consuming fascination to the young and single local blokes who are mostly the sons of farmers and likely to inherit the farms. Half of the young ladies who arrive in Gunnery Bay as fresh-faced transients will never leave. They will, instead, become experts at animal husbandry, child rearing and unpaid community lynchpinning. They will become the very backbone of the town that they had hoped would be, at most, a three-year sojourn.

The quickest way for any young transient to be accepted into Gunnery Bay society is to join at least one sports team. There are quite a few offerings. Football, cricket, tennis and netball are the major recruiters but there are also opportunities if you show the slightest interest in table tennis, darts, bowls, 8-ball or yachting.

There is a badminton club but if you join that, you'll be branded as a dickhead. Not because the sport of badminton is in any way outlandish – it's just that the resident members all happen to be dickheads.

*

Young Brian Grillitsch took his place behind the counter at the Gunnery Bay branch of NatCom Rural (formerly Nationwide Community Bank). This was not where he'd expected to be. Well, he'd expected to be in a bank – but not in a bank in Gunnery Bay. It had never occurred to him that he might find himself posted to a place that didn't exist in his *Gregory's Street Directory*.

Misfortune in the shape of the bank's board had ambushed young Brian by deciding to expand its rural division and to cleverly rebrand its country branches as NatCom Rural. All current trainees were to receive a final three months of intensive training in matters agricultural before receiving a mandatory three-year rural posting.

Coincidentally, Faraday's Stock & Station Agency in Gunnery Bay became Faraday Farming, and Abbott's Trucking & Transport became ATTrans. These changes in business branding followed a recent trend towards snappy letterheads that didn't actually tell you what business they were in.

So young Brian Grillitsch, who at that time had little interest in banking and even less in pastoral pursuits, became learned in all things rural from stubble-burning to stock prices – the four-legged sort.

That he could absorb such unlikely bumf came as no surprise. Brian was an information sponge. Inside Brian's average-sized head sat a seemingly unfillable brain with an unfailing memory. Any fact, story, gossip or conversation that happened anywhere near Brian's brain got filed away and stored forever. Even stuff that Brian-the-Bloke didn't find interesting or tasteful got absorbed by Brian-the-Brain. In fact, there were times when Brian-the-Brain directed Brian-the-Bloke towards even more stuff to absorb. Outdated women's magazines in waiting rooms were favourite. For the rest of his life, his brain would recall biscuit recipes and tips on stain removal that he, Brian-the-Bloke, would likely never need.

Thus he became the most outstanding trainee of 1969 with the paradoxical prediction that he had a rainbow future in banking. They couldn't know that this young man had only applied for a bank job because it paid reasonably well and it got his parents off his back.

So both his brain and his parents were happy with Brian's decision to enter the world of banking. It was a career with a solid future and, more importantly, it should also mean that he might start paying his own way – somewhere else.

A career in banking might also distract him from the fixation that had obsessed him for the two years since completing high school – the guitar.

So impressive were his final year results that Brian could have taken his pick of university courses. He'd considered several, including pharmacy, visual arts and geology but lost interest on discovering that none of them included guitar.

He'd joined, and subsequently left, a dozen half-baked rock bands all of which valued volume over virtuosity and playlists predicated on the potential to attract girls. No one cared how well Brian could copy Syd Barrett so long as he played it loudly and seductively. He had nothing against attracting girls. Seduction and amassing piles of money were high on his list of reasons for playing the guitar.

Brian's brain, while super-efficient at storage, wasn't so hot at operating the rest of his body. It was, for example, hopeless at directing his legs to run, or kick, or dance or his arms to catch, or throw, or hit anything. Fingers, however, seemed to be within its grasp – so to speak – and Brian had become adept at fingering his way around a fretboard.

By year 11, he had left Hank Marvin far behind and was well on the way to mastering most of George Harrison, Eric Clapton, Syd Barrett and Jimi Hendrix. So, while his parents had seen banking as a secure and sagacious career path, Brian had seen it as a means to an end. And that end was to be an open-shirted, tight-leathered and wealthy guitarist at whom other young men gaped in wonder and young women threw intimate undergarments. He'd almost tasted it with a band called the Wizards, who were a cut above. Occasionally he spoke on the phone with Stitch, their bassist. Apparently their current lead guitarist was crap.

Of course, Brian's plan was predicated on him working in the big smoke. Somewhere with live music venues, rock concerts, record shops and bands with – in the music vernacular – axemen. Somewhere with more than one television channel and more than one radio station. Somewhere that had moved beyond Bill Haley. Somewhere that wasn't Gunnery Bay.

*

The bank manager was a decent bloke. The polished wooden nameplate on his door read 'Walter Hudson' but around Gunnery Bay they called him Bomber. Shortish, roundish and baldish, he had, apparently, been a bloody good footballer, in the nuggetty mould, who could have played state league but for the uncertainties of a dicky knee.

He'd been on hand when young Brian Grillitsch pulled his smoking EK Holden station wagon into the kerb outside the bank in the early evening of a January Friday. After a brief welcome, he'd led his new clerk to Mrs Cynthia Harrison's boarding house, made the introductions and helped the lad carry his stuff in from the car.

Mrs Harrison was a widow of some eight years and looked like she hadn't shaved since her husband had passed on nor stuck to their Live Longer Diet Plan. She was, in a Sherman tank kind of way, large, grey and formidable with a high-pitched, grinding kind of voice like an oil-starved gearbox. She didn't help with the unloading but held the screen door open so as to look helpful but actually so as to get a good gander

at the incoming luggage and so form an early first impression of her
new boarder. She'd get a more complete impression when Brian was at
the bank on Monday and she could sift through his room at leisure.
The two guitar cases and the amplifier didn't go unnoticed by either
Walter Hudson or Mrs Harrison ,who shook her head and tsk, tsk,
tsked as they passed by.

She'd had two rooms available for rent, one already occupied by a
young chap named Peter Brookman, who worked at Faraday Farming.
The tank landlady made quite a to-do about having kept a serving of
shepherd's pie warm despite the fact that her new boarder had arrived
an hour past the dinner bell. Brian was, by nature, a placid and quite
well-mannered lad but, having just driven his reluctant, non-air-con-
ditioned EK Holden through five hours of January heat to arrive at the
arse end of the universe, he found himself thinking of Mrs Harrison as
a total shit.

Mr Walter 'Bomber' Hudson had suggested that he pick up Brian
in the morning and introduce him to Gunnery Bay. Then he left his
new clerk to a serving of dried-out-looking shepherd's pie while Mrs
Harrison sat opposite at the Laminex table and recited a list of house
procedures. Laundry in the basket by Thursday mornings and no noise
after 9.30 p.m. Wet towels left on the towel rails and no noise after 9.30
p.m. Toothbrushes kept in bedrooms and no noise after 9.30 p.m.
Lunches not provided and no noise after 9.30 p.m. No smoking or
drinking and no noise after 9.30p.m. The two guitars and the amplifier
seemed to be playing heavily on Mrs Harrison's mind.

The bank manager had also had a few doubtful thoughts about
Brian Grillitsch as he drove away. NatCom Rural had been a reliable
source of recruits to the Gunners footy team and the Gunners cricket
team, neither of which were noted for originality in selecting their club's
name. Putting that local idiosyncrasy aside, young Brian had the sort
of physique more suited to a pipe cleaner than a player. He'd last about
three minutes into a footy game even if he was sitting on the bench.
On a cricket pitch, he'd look like a fourth stump.

Bomber Hudson knew the importance of community acceptance. Life in Gunnery Bay could be brilliant for those young transients who fitted in but miserable for those who didn't. And fitting in usually meant playing sport. You didn't have to be great at sport, although it helped. You just had to get dirty, throw a few punches in support of your mates, abuse the ump, shower together, have a few beers afterward and get invited to other shenanigans.

Brian's predecessor had been a solid defender on the footy field and a more than useful fast bowler. His name was Bruce. He'd fitted in and enjoyed four good years in Gunnery Bay.

The only other bank employee was a local lass named Connie Long. She hid behind an IBM electric typewriter on her tidy desk and only served at the counter on Mondays or whenever the customers were more than one deep. Always cheerful, Connie was that person which every office relies upon to answer the phone, type the letters, order supplies, file documents and put her finger on any information required with one minute's notice. She was also captain of the Gunners netball team. Bomber knew that he had a little gem in Connie, which is why he, the manager, always made the coffee for her, the secretary.

Come Mondays and you'd find Connie front and centre alongside Bruce behind the counter while the male customers dissected the footy game and the ladies of Gunnery Bay discussed how Connie had dissected the opposition netball players. And Bomber kept the coffee coming to his junior employees and just loved being the bank manager at Gunnery Bay.

But now Bruce had been transferred and replaced by a beanpole. A beanpole who was unlikely to draw sports fans into the bank. Bomber Hudson, now a troubled bank manager, spent an uneasy Friday evening.

*

Saturday dawned like it would start hot and just get hotter. Lucky then that Bomber had only recently taken delivery of his Rover 3500. It was a fairly exotic set of wheels for Gunnery Bay but Bomber reckoned that it fitted the image of a bank manager and, besides, it had air conditioning.

He took young Brian firstly to the bank, which was much, much smaller than the grandiose, columned edifice in which Brian had trained back in the big smoke. The columnless Gunnery Bay branch didn't have, for example, any tellers' booths – just a small counter with enough room, at a pinch, for four customers at a time. The manager's office, off to one side, had three doors. One opened into the customer area, one connected the bank with the manager's residence and the third door opened into the staff area behind the counter.

From there, they took a familiarising cruise of the town.

Gunnery Bay is a long town. It starts with the hospital at one end of the bay and ends with the caravan park at the other. It is only four streets deep. Closest to the ocean is, logically, the Esplanade, which separates the beach from the Gunners Arms Hotel, Calibre Kiosk, Gunnery Bay Motel, Gunnery Bay Yacht Club and U-catch'em (formerly Ted's Tackle & Sporting Goods. Fresh bait available). The foreshore is, obviously, the focus of the town and of the holidaymakers who were in crimson-skinned abundance as Bomber idled along the Esplanade and offered a chatty commentary.

A white-sanded beach slid gently into shallow green waters, making it hopeless for beach fishers but ideal for kids to frolic safely. Couch grass had been sown in the strip between the sand and the Esplanade and it was studded for its entire length, between hospital and camping ground, with picnic tables and Norfolk Island pine trees.

From the precise centre of the beach's arc, the jetty thrust out beyond the sandy shallows to reach the blue water. Most of the old screw piles, against which grain clippers had once tied, had been removed for the benefit of fisherfolk. The rusted sign which insisted that there be 'No Jumping or Diving from Jetty' did little more than suggest the exciting possibilities of jumping or diving from the jetty.

The Esplanade was an essay in chiaroscuro, of counterchange between the white glare of raw sunlight and the deep blue shadows of pine trees and wide verandas. It was a picture just made for postcards. Brian, unappreciative of visual poetry, had found it depressing.

Commercial Road, one back from the foreshore, boasted the Cannon Fodder Café, the Target Takeaway Restaurant, Faraday Farming, NatCom Rural and a whole row of living-in-the-past businesses that had yet to rebrand themselves and could still be identified as a pharmacy, a ladies' and men's clothing, a shoe shop and leather worker, a big general store, a post office, the police station, a newsagent, a garage with petrol bowsers and the council chambers/library. Clippers Lady's and Gent's Hair Salon pre-dated the trend to kitschy branding so was excused any potential criticism.

Further from the sea, along Education Road, stood, predictably, the area school, the kindergarten, two churches, the council yards, sports fields, showgrounds and a dozen houses. The rest of suburbia spread along the fourth and cleverly named Fourth Street. From there on it was wheat, sheep, silos and scrub.

As they passed the school, Bomber swung the Rover through a set of impressive stone gateposts and past a little shed that looked like a sentry box. 'Just need to check up on something.' He glanced at Brian. 'Won't take a sec.'

It was the town oval, shared with the school and surrounded by the netball courts, the tennis courts and the cricket nets. A big corrugated-iron hall was the obvious centrepiece of the Gunnery Bay Agricultural and Horticultural Show Society, which, mercifully, had yet to become the Gunbaghoss.

There was a cricket game under way – a junior cricket game. You could tell they were juniors because they all wore crisply pressed and blindingly white cricket creams and neat baggy greens – green and tan being the Gunners club colours. More senior grades of country cricketers tend to turn out in whatever's hanging over the end of the bed when they wake after Friday-night-pre-game-strategy meetings in the pub. Juniors, or juniors' mums, are much more attentive of appearance.

'The under-fourteens,' explained Bomber as he pulled up in the shade of a big pine tree. 'C'mon, you might as well start meeting a few blokes.'

A small group of adults, some standing, others sitting on folding chairs, were gathered in the shade of a small grandstand. They were surrounded by the paraphernalia vital to junior sport: Eskys, sports bags, drink bottles and oranges. More senior grades of country cricketers tend to turn up with nothing more than a can of Coke, a pie and the trust that they can borrow everything from a teammate: gloves, bats, prewarmed protectors. This is true mateship.

Another group were gathered a little further along. Their group included lots of lightweight, creamed cricketers wearing baggy blues. The opposition – who were batting.

As they approached the first group, there was a high-pitched appeal from the players. It must have been successful, because one of the baggyblues began dragging his bat disconsolately towards the boundary as the baggy greens celebrated by slapping each other.

'G'day, Singer. How's it going?' asked Bomber of a tall young man who was applauding the dismissal.

Singer looked over the shoulder of a seated woman as if to consult the score sheet. She was a small and slightly built woman with a curly mop of bleached-ginger hair and deeply tanned face which spoke of too much time in the sun. The crêpe paper texture around her mouth spoke of too many smokes. She snarled. Singer withdrew.

'Three for twenty-eight,' she rasped.

'Not bad, Bomber. They're three for twenty-eight. Young Tel's taken all three wickets.'

'Good oh,' responded Bomber. 'I reckon young Tel might be ready for a run in the seconds next season.' He put a hand on Brian's shoulder. 'Singer Long, this is Brian Grillitsch. He'll be starting at the bank on Monday.'

Singer thrust out a hand and nearly wrenched Brian's fingers off. 'G'day, Brian. Nice to meet you. Are you a batsman or a bowler?'

Brian surreptitiously reorganised his fingers. 'Nah, neither. I've not played cricket since primary school.' He didn't add that cricket balls, like Singer's handshake, were not compatible with guitarists' fingers.

'Ah well, maybe you can come out for a bit of a knock on Thursday. We train over there, in the nets.'

He pointed to the cyclone wire enclosures where four smallish lads were recreating the gritty stand of Redpath and Walters against the Pommy attack – the only bright spot in a test match loss of two hundred and ninety-nine runs.

'So, all set for this afternoon, Singer?' interjected Bomber. 'Got someone to umpire? A scorer? How's Johnno's wrist?'

'Yair. All set, mate. Johnno was turning them a mile last Thursday. Marty's teed up to umpire and Joy here will see to the scoring. Right, Joy?'

The seated lady added two runs to the baggy blues total, looked up and snapped. 'Well, there's no one else putting their bloody hand up.'

'Right, I'll see yer later,' smiled Bomber in the face of an awkward moment. He edged away from the lady who didn't seem to be happy in her work. Then he led Brian back to the Rover. 'Big match this arvo,' he explained. 'Win this and we're in the grand final.' He opened the car door and looked over the roof to Brian. 'I'm the president of the club. For my sins.'

It had taken a bit over an hour to complete their tour of the town. As he sat back in the Rover, Brian was fairly certain of two things. Firstly, he was unlikely to ever get lost in this puny town of only four streets; and secondly, his new boss, Mr Walter 'Bomber' Hudson, was one of the nicest blokes he'd ever come across.

This was confirmed when his boss consulted his watch and said, 'Eleven-thirty, the wife's expecting us for lunch at midday. Connie's coming for lunch…' He saw Brian's questioning glance and added, 'Connie Long…Singer's sister…your co-worker…our secretary, receptionist, filing clerk. You name it, she does it. I could drop dead tomorrow and no one'd notice, because Connie runs the place. You'll love her. Everybody else does.'

The Hudsons – Walter, Jillian and young daughter Carole – lived in the official bank manager's residence, which was behind and attached to the bank. Just as the postmaster lived in the postmaster's residence behind and attached to the post office, and the newsagent lived in the newsagent's residence which, well, didn't need explaining.

Mrs Hudson – Jillian – was a smidge taller than her husband, but then most of Gunnery Bay was a smidge taller than Walter. Slender, with close-cropped dark hair and deep green eyes, she was also, again like most of Gunnery Bay, a lot more attractive than her husband.

Bomber made the introductions and then sat Brian at the kitchen table while he fetched cups from the crockery cupboard and Jillian put on the kettle. Brian noticed that the slender Jillian wasn't quite so slender in profile and figured that their young daughter Carole was expecting a playmate. At the moment, the toddler was intently scrutinising their visitor from behind the safety of a high chair.

This was nice. Brian took in the old-style kitchen, probably little-changed since the house was built – when? Eighty years ago? A hundred? The louvred windows over the sink looked out to a wide veranda with, beyond, a grassed yard barely big enough to contain the rotary clothes hoist. A painted-plank door at one end of the veranda would be the laundry. Through an inside door he could see what was obviously the living room but also, unexpectedly, a baby grand piano.

Bomber noticed his noticing and began, 'Ah, yes, the baby grand. That's Jillian's. She used to be… Ah, here's Connie.'

A young lady, apparently Connie, had come in through the back door saying, 'Knock, knock' but without actually knocking.

It was a familiarity welcomed by Jillian, who gave her a quick hug and then told her to 'Grab a cup and park yourself.'

'Hello, boss,' said the young lady to Bomber, who smiled and responded.

'Gidday, Connie. How's things?' and, before she could elucidate him on how things were, he added, 'This is Brian Grillitsch, our new bloke. Brian, this is Connie.'

She reached over the table and took his hand in a grip not much gentler than Singer's. 'Hello, Brian,' she said in a voice much softer than her handshake. 'Welcome to Gunnery Bay. Did you have a good drive over here? Where are you staying?'

Brian sorted through his fingers before sorting through the questions. 'Er…yes…not a bad drive. I'm…er…staying at Mrs Harrison's place.'

Connie screwed up her attractive face – and it was a very attractive face. Like Jillian, she wore her hair cut shortish but, unlike her hostess, Connie's was blonde. She was wearing a white tennis outfit which enhanced her athleticism and tanned legs, which Brian tried not to notice too obviously. 'Hm…right…Harrison the Harridan,' she mused. 'That'll be…interesting for you.' She turned to Jillian, who was chopping something at the sink. 'Need a hand, Jillian?'

'No thanks, Connie. All under control. We'll eat now so's you can get off to tennis.' She started laying plates of cold meats, shelled prawns, potato salad and curried eggs on the table. 'So tuck in everyone.'

*

The meal was something of a fact-finding mission for both sides. The visiting side learned a lot about his new neighbourhood – mostly about local personalities, local gossip and various character assassinations. Useful stuff for someone who would undoubtedly be required to attend to the bank accounts of those personalities, gossips and assassinated characters. The local side learned quite a lot about the visiting side: where had he lived back in the big smoke? What school did he go to? What sports did he play? None. A moment's silence. Then, did he have any interests outside of banking? Yes, the guitar.

Ah, the guitar: common ground, music. Mrs Hudson – Jillian – played the aforementioned piano and Connie knew her way around

the clarinet and the alto saxophone. In fact, the two ladies made up half
of the GeeBees which, explained Connie, were the initials of Gunnery
Bay. The other half were Digby Cole on drums and Merv Pugnall on
double bass.

'We're playing tonight out at Butler's Well,' enthused Jillian. 'The
monthly 60/40. You should come out there and meet a few people,
Brian.' She turned to her husband. 'Whaderyer reckon, Wal? Connie
and I have to get out there and set up a bit early. You could pick up
Brian and bring him out a bit later.'

'No worries,' responded Bomber, who was, apparently, Wal when
at home. 'Whaderyer reckon, Brian? Fancy a quick quickstep? Tell yer
what, they put on a bloody good supper.'

'Great," said Brian not sure what was meant by a Butler's Well, a
monthly 60/40 or a quick quickstep. The bloody good supper sounded
OK. Besides – anything sounded better than a Saturday night at home
with Mrs Harrison the Harridan.

*

Butler's Well turned out to be a corrugated-iron hall, a red phone box,
two street lights and six houses clustered around a dirt crossroads about
twelve kilometres inland from Gunnery Bay. It was as brightly lit as
could be provided by one phone box, two street lights and a string of
coloured globes draped festively across the front of the corrugated-iron
hall. The veranda lights of three houses added to the glare and a yellow
school bus parked in a driveway added a splash of carnival colour.

There were about forty cars parked randomly around the hall as
Bomber drew up in the Rover. More were arriving. This was, evidently,
a big gig. Brian was, at once, both intrigued and slightly terrified. Intrigued by the popularity of what seemed to be nothing more than a
knees-up in a tin shed and terrified by the prospect of 60/40 music,
which, Bomber explained, meant 60% traditional dances like waltzes
and military two-steps and suchlike, and 40% modern. which, appar-

ently, meant stuff like rock and roll and the twist and suchlike. The twist, my God, on piano, clarinet, drums and double bass! Here was hoping that the supper truly was bloody good.

*

It was bloody good – and in abundance. Everybody brought at least one platter of food and there seemed to be a competitive element to the presentation of the tucker. There weren't, for example, any cheese sandwiches. But there was one platter of Roquefort and chili chutney, another of Stilton and chives and yet another of Camembert with cranberry. Nor were there any ordinary scones – there were pumpkin and curry scones, paprika and apricot scones and Parmesan scones. Cakes and slices jostled with lamingtons on trestle tables that hugged the entire length of one wall.

But the music – the music – God, it was truly awful. The little quartet, the GeeBees, played pretty well – very well, in fact. But the stuff that they were playing – there was no getting around it – it was bloody terrible.

Bomber led Brian to the trestles, where they piled a modest selection of tucker onto paper plates and then found seats close to the little raised stage. They had time for just two dainty smoked salmon sandwiches before Bomber was hauled onto the dance floor by a rather large lady who obviously wasn't interested in waiting for a ladies' choice and wasn't going to accede to a refusal. From behind the upright piano, Jillian announced a Canadian barn dance and the GeeBees broke into 'Opus One'. Left alone with two plates of tucker, Brian nibbled on a parmesan and capsicum scone while he focused on the band. He wasn't familiar with 'Opus One', which predated him by nearly a decade, but it didn't take long for him to appreciate that each member of the GeeBees was a pretty fair musician and that they clicked OK as a quartet. Jillian on piano, Connie on sax and Merv on double bass took turns with the melody, while Digby on drums added a few interesting little flourishes to the boringly steady dance beat. It was a competent performance but they might just as well have beaten saucepans with wooden spoons for all the dancers cared.

The 60% of waltzes, and polkas, and military two-steps were as was to be expected: dead ordinary; functional; good to dance to. The floor was crowded. The 40% modern were a struggle. Piano, clarinet, drums and double bass isn't a combo that works well with Chubby Checker – as if anything could. Nor did Gene Vincent or Paul Anka fare much better, despite some really good solos that were wasted on the crowd. They made a fair fist of the Seekers and Beatles numbers but, by and large, most of the crowd spent 60% of their time dancing waltzes and 40% at the tucker on the trestle tables.

The short trip back to Gunnery Bay with Bomber was – awkward. The bank manager was bubbling. He'd had a great night – lots of tucker, joking with clients, dancing with their wives, rejoicing in the Gunners' innings of eight for two hundred and-ninety-three declared and then to already have the opposition at two for seventeen earlier that after-noon. It didn't get much better.

'So, young Brian,' he was tapping out a beat on the steering wheel – could be 'Tennessee Waltz', could be 'Lucy in the Sky with Diamonds' …hard to tell – 'what did you think of the GeeBees? Pretty good, aren't they?'

He thought, 'Bloody terrible,' but he answered, 'Yes, pretty good. The crowd certainly likes 'em.'

'I'll say they do.' He slipped into a four-four on the steering wheel. Possibly Cliff Richard. 'There's a 60/40 every month out at Butler's Well, always a good crowd. They play at weddings and suchlike too.' He hummed a few tuneless bars of, possibly, Duke Ellington. 'Tell you what, you should bring your guitar around one night and have a jam with Jillian. We'll invite young Connie as well. Yes, that's what we'll do. I'll talk to Jillian. Pencil in next Friday.'

Brian had nothing to say. They pulled up outside the Harridan's, er, Harrison's.

'OK,' said Bomber. 'That's been quite an introduction for you on your first day. So we'll see you at eight-thirty sharp on Monday.' Then, as Brian opened his door, 'Best tiptoe from here. Mrs Harrison doesn't like any noise after nine-thirty.'

*

Sunday was fairly ordinary. Breakfast set the tone: ordinary cereal, ordinary toast and canned jam. Then he sorted out his room and decided that it would be undies in the top drawer and socks in the second. Then, to get last night's music out of his head, he played a few Hendrix riffs on the acoustic guitar before walking to the Esplanade to buy ordinary bland fish and ordinary limp chips at Calibre's Kiosk. But for the excess salt and vinegar, they would have been tasteless. They were wrapped in pages from the sports section of Saturday's *Express* – more cricket.

He sat on a wooden bench which looked out to sea and was provided by the Gunnery Bay Lions Club. Twenty seagulls descended on the possibility of a feed but Brian was in no mood to part with a chip, no matter how limp and ordinary.

It was, to anybody but Brian, a perfect holiday Sunday. A light sea breeze moderated the temperature but not so much as to discourage the sort of frolicking and romping expected of visiting holidaymakers. Delighted shrieks of pure joy came from the crystal-clear, shimmering green water while boisterous beach cricket appeals came from the pristine white sands of the gently sloping beach. Brian found it all a bit depressing.

He finished most of his ordinary bland fish and ordinary limp chips and stood up. He was about to chuck the final limp chips into a brightly painted yellow bin also provided by the Gunnery Bay Lions Club when, because he was, at heart, a decent young chap, he threw them to the seagulls, who had stuck around because they had perceived that he was, at heart, a decent young chap.

He walked back to the Harridan's – er, Harrison's – boarding house and moved his undies into the third drawer.

Holidaymakers don't usually rise early but, on this particular Monday, they'd conspired to remind Brian that they were still recreating while he wasn't. There seemed to be hundreds of them frolicking and romping all over Gunnery Bay as Brian trudged to his first day of clerking at NatCom Rural. His first decision, other than that involving his undies drawer, was to never again approach the bank from the Esplanade. All that frolicking and romping just made him more pissed off.

He met Connie on the bank steps. She was depressingly cheerful and he, because he was, at heart, a decent young chap, did his best to match her smiles. Bomber entered from the manager's residence and then opened the bank's front door from the inside. They stepped inside and he locked the door behind them. The bank didn't open for business for another hour.

'Morning, morning,' he enthused. 'First order of business…coffee. Brian, how do you take it?'

Bank managers making coffee was outside of Brian's experience. He hesitated, 'Er…white with two, thanks.'

As Bomber headed for the kettle, Connie leaned against the new boy and side-mouthed, 'Best boss you'll ever work for, mate. Play it straight with Bomber and he'll see you right. You landed with your bum in the butter when you got posted to Gunnery Bay.'

This didn't accord with his impressions of Gunnery Bay thus far: Harridan's boarding house, obsession with sport, crappy 60/40 music and loud, sunburnt frolickers and rompers frolicking and romping all over the place.

Connie sensed his doubts. 'Give it a chance, mate. Think of all the shit places you could have been sent to.'

He couldn't.

She shifted away as Bomber approached with three mugs.

'Here we go.' He passed around the coffee and they sat around Connie's desk.

There was some discussion of tennis, and cricket and 60/40 dancing. Brian sat and sipped and watched Bomber and Connie bounce off each other. You'd never know that they were boss and bottle-washer.

'Right,' announced Bomber when he had drained his mug. 'First up, Brian, we'll crack the safe and get out the teller's tray so's you can count the cash and check it against the ledgers. I'm assuming that you've done all this stuff in training?'

'Yes, most of it,' responded the new boy. 'But I've never opened a safe before. The manager or head teller always drew the tellers' trays and checked them.'

'Well, around here you're the teller and the head teller and the only teller…so you do it all. Come through to my office and we'll run through the formalities.' He got up and gathered the mugs – apparently this bank manager did the dishes as well.

Connie flicked the new boy a wink.

*

Bomber spent most of the morning alongside Brian at the counter. Not because he felt the need to scrutinise the new teller but because someone had to be on hand to analyse the Gunners' innings of eight for two hundred and ninety-three declared with the opposition sitting on two for seventeen in reply. Apparently, Johnno's wrist had fully recovered, because he'd spun out both wickets.

The steady stream of customers made ridiculously small transactions: withdraw ten dollars, deposit twelve dollars, get a bank cheque for three dollars, cash a lottery win of two dollars eighty-five. The real interest was, of course, in the new transient whose predecessor had been Bruce, a solid defender on the footy field and a more than useful fast bowler.

Most came away disappointed in young Brian, who they thought too thin, very unathletic and wearing his brown hair a bit longer than one might expect of a bank teller. Bomber and Connie went to great lengths to convince their customers that Brian was a most welcome addition to the staff.

'Top of his training seminar,' whispered the manager. 'Lucky to get him.'

'That's wonderful – but what position does he play?'

Then something odd happened just before lunch. Merv Pugnall, the stock manager at Faraday Farming and also the double bass player in the GeeBees, came in to deposit seven dollars in small change. Given that the stock manager was unlikely to have sold many sheep or cattle for seven dollars in small change, it was fairly obvious that Merv was being nosy. He'd met Brian briefly at the 60/40 and hadn't been terribly impressed.

Bomber greeted him at the counter and reintroduced the new chap. Brian took Merv's jam-jar of small change, gently poured it onto a green felt cloth and started sorting coins as the two men discussed – what else? Cricket.

This would be the twenty-third time that Brian had heard about the Gunners' innings of eight for two hundred and ninety-three declared with the opposition sitting on two for seventeen in reply with Johnno's wrist spinning out both wickets. He tuned out and concentrated on the one- and two-cent coins.

But, apparently, another cricket game had started last Thursday in Melbourne. And, apparently, there had been some spirited batting and a bit of controversy.

Merv was keen to engage in a lengthy analysis – sheep and cattle sales were slow in January. 'Not a bad start on Thursday,' he opened . 'Stacky and Lawrie made an opening half-century...'

'Sixty-four,' said Brian unconsciously. 'Sixty-five...sixty-six...sixty-seven...oh, bugger.' And then had to start counting all over again as the two men looked at him. 'One...two...three...

'Yair, right...sixty-four.' nodded Merv and turned back to Bomber. 'Good to see young Chappell rack up a ton...'

'Hundred and eleven,' offered Brian. 'Hundred and twelve...hundred and thirteen…oh, bugger…' Then sighed and started on the five-cent coins again. 'Five…ten…fifteen…'

Again, Merv and Bomber stared at him. But he kept on counting.

'Yair,' said Bomber. 'That's right…a hundred and eleven. Marshy was a bit stiff when Lawry declared while he was on ninety-odd…'

'Ninety-two,' said Brian. And then, seemingly to himself, 'Declared at nine for four hundred and ninety-three…ninety-four…ninety-five… oh, bugger…ten…twenty…thirty…'

This brought the conversation to a close. Even Connie had left her typing and was studying Brian with a bemused expression.

Bomber put a hand on his shoulder. 'Oi, mate. How come you know so much about the fifth test?'

'Fifth…sixth…seventh… Eh? What?'

'The fifth test,' repeated Bomber. 'How come you know all the scores?'

Brian looked totally puzzled. 'I don't know all the…I'm not…' Then it dawned. 'Oh shit,' he thought, 'those bloody sports pages…with the bloody bland fish and limp chips.' His super-absorbent brain had mem-orised the scores while he wasn't paying attention. He collected himself and stumbled, 'Oh, y'know. Just read 'em…y'know…in the paper…'

'That's quite a trick, young fella,' said Merv. 'Did you memorise the whole scoreboard? What did Dougie Walters make?'

'Fifty-five,' answered Brian without thinking. 'No…I didn't mem-orise the whole sco– Just a few things stuck…y'know…in my head… y'know…'

'How about Willis?' interrupted Merv.

'Three for seventy-three off twenty overs with five-maidens,' snapped back Brian. And then mumbled to himself, 'Whatever that means…'

Connie could see that their new bloke was flustered. She looked at the big clock on the wall. 'Lunchtime, boss. Want me to shut the door.'

Bomber took the hint and turned to Merv. 'Sorry, mate. Have to shut up shop. Bank rules. Do you want Brian to organise a deposit slip for that jarful? He could drop it around later.'

'Er…yair, all right,' said Merv, still studying the new teller curiously. 'Yair, right… No, no, don't bother. I'll drop in after lunch and sign it. Yair, see yer later, Bomber. See yer, Connie.' He gave Brian one more baffled look and left.

*

Brian decided that a hamburger from the Target Takeaway Restaurant might be a better bet than another serving of bland fish and limp chips from Calibre's Kiosk. Besides, it would mean that he wouldn't need to walk down to the Esplanade, where most of the over-eager frolicking and romping was going on.

The Target Takeaway Restaurant offered an impressive range of hamburger variants. He opted for the Hawaiian and, while the cook went looking for a can opener, ducked into the newsagents and bought an *Express*.

The hamburger, while unlikely to enhance any respectable Hawaiian Luau, wasn't too bad. Brian sat at an outside table and, for the first time in his life, opened the *Express* to the sports section.

The fifth test looked to be heading for a draw. The Poms had replied to the Aussies' nine for four ninety-three declared with three ninety-two including forty-two sundries – mostly due to Thommo's wild deliveries while taking three for a hundred and ten. At close of play yesterday, the Aussies, in their second dig, were one for fifty-five. Highlights included centuries to Chappell, Luckhurst and D'Oliveira.

Brian-the-Bloke had little idea of what he was reading but Brian-the-Brain loved statistics. Cricket, it seemed, was as much about statistics as it was about hitting a ball around an oval. Statistics were so precise, so – ordered. They could be pigeonholed beautifully within the filing cabinet that was Brian-the-Brain's skull. As Brian-the-Bloke ran his finger down the printed batting orders, Brian-the-Brain sorted, catalogued, cross-referenced and then added little asterisks to highlight potential discussion topics such as Lawry leaving Marsh stranded eight runs short of a century.

When the bank opened that afternoon, there was a new cricket oracle standing behind the counter.

*

At the far end of Commercial Road stood the Gunnery Bay Town Hall, which boasted a photogenic neoclassical façade and a lot of plain brickwork around the back. The semi-attached library was plain brick and managed by a plain librarian named, appropriately, Mrs Thelma Pikestaff.

Mrs Pikestaff had been widowed for some thirty years and was one of the boarding house cartel who picked up a tidy supplementary income from her three boarders: two young teachers who shared her house and one rather more senior gentleman who had bached in her converted shed for over ten years and who, many chose to deliciously believe, had a dark past and one slipper under MrsPikestaff's bed.

The fifty-something-year-old Mrs Thelma Pikestaff did nothing to discourage such rumours because they gave her a piquant bad girl notoriety usually accorded to painted floozies. Mrs Pikestaff, unpainted librarian, sometimes wondered what fate might have proffered had she left Gunnery Bay for the life of a painted floozy in the big smoke.

Brian was unaware of Mrs Pikestaff's musings when he burst through the library door just minutes before she was due to lock up. Her 'Shhhhhhhhhhhhh' was an automatic reflex. There was no one else in the room and hadn't been since Norma Truscott had returned *Twenty Raffia Lampshades for You to Make* and *Lust by Lamplight* just after lunch.

'I'm just about to close the library,' she informed the unknown young man. Then, not unkindly, 'Can I help you with anything?'

'Yes, please. Do you have anything on cricket scores? Test match results? That sort of thing?'

Thelma knew every book in her charge intimately. She'd been glad to note the return of *Lust by Lamplight* from Norma, who had borrowed it at least five times in the past six months. It now automatically fell open at pages 37, 88 and 214.

Without the need to consult her index, she declared, 'I've got *50 years of Australian Cricket* and *Cricket Lists 1900–1968* and I've got Wisden's *Almanacs* for most of the past ten years.'

'Great,' enthused Brian. 'Can I borrow all of them?'

'Well, you could if you were a registered borrower.' She smiled benignly. 'But I'm sure that you don't have a library card because I don't know who you are.'

'Oh…yes,' said Brian. 'My name's Brian Grillitsch. I've just started at the bank. I'm boarding at Mrs Harrid– er…Harrison's.'

As a member of the widows-who-own-large-and-largely-empty-houses cartel, Mrs Thelma Pikestaff made it her business to know who boarded with whom and how much rent was paid by whom to whom. She and Cynthia Harrison not only belonged to the same cartel, they were also quite good friends and regularly attended social events together. 'Ah…yes…Mr Grillitsch. You're staying with Cynthia. Welcome to Gunnery Bay. Now, you've rather caught me on the hop. I must get home and get dinner started.' She hesitated. 'Look, I'll tell you what I'll do. You can take the Wisdens home tonight providing that you drop in tomorrow and fill out the library card application. Then you can borrow anything you like.' She paused, enquiring eyebrow raised. And then, because it was cricket, she raised a finger and asked, 'How's that?'

'That's wonderful,' he gushed as he followed her to a shelf, where Dewey announced, '796; Arts & Recreation; Athletics, Sports and Outdoor Games'.

'Thanks very much,'' as she handed him a small pile of Wisden's *Almanacs*. 'I'll be in at lunchtime tomorrow.'

She followed him outside and locked the door behind them.

*

Brian walked to work next morning secure in the certainty that no one in Gunnery Bay had more knowledge of the 1969–70 tours of South Africa and India, the West Indian visitors in 1968–69, the tour of England earlier in 1968 and the rout of the Indians when they toured Australia in the summer of 1967–68.

Merv Pugnall, who had his own collection of Wisdens, had spent much of the evening concocting a list of cricketing questions to stump the new lad. By sheer coincidence, he had found another large jar of coins that had perched on the fridge for years. He divided the coins into six smaller jars which now suddenly needed depositing – one at a time. He was on the bank's doorstep when Bomber opened for business.

'Morning, young Brian,' he smiled. 'Would you believe I've just found another jar?' Then, almost without pause, 'Best figures for Mallett against India…?'

Immediately, 'Five for ninety-one off twenty-five overs,' and then – a little cherry on the cake – 'seven sundries.'

Merv dumped the jar and muttered his way out of the bank.

Fifteen minutes later and, 'Unbelievable…another jar just turned up… Most runs last summer – Richards or Barlow?'

This took Brian-the-Brain a fraction longer. 'Richards…er…five hundred and eight. Barlow…hang on…three hundred and sixty.'

Merv consulted a tiny set of numbers written surreptitiously on his cuff. Then, muttering, 'Bloody clever bugger,' he departed to consult his Wisdens and to find yet another jar of small change.

At lunchtime, Brian-the-Brain propelled Brian-the-Bloke back to the library to fill out a borrowing card while Mrs Thelma Pikestaff fetched every cricketing reference from the shelves. The young man was the most enthusiastic borrower she'd helped in years, if you didn't count Norma Truscott, whose borrowing enthusiasms were suspect.

*

By nine-thirty on Friday morning, the queue outside the NatCom Rural wound down Commercial Road as far as Faraday Farming. Most were blokes and most were clutching jars of small change. Many appeared to have surreptitious writing on their cuffs.

Both Bomber and Connie were pressed into totalling up piddling amounts of coinage while their customers tried to out-statistic young Brian. A few – a very few – successfully stumped him but only by asking obscure questions that didn't really qualify as statistical. Owen Jones, for example, snuck in a question about the cost of the BBC broadcasting rights from the MCC in 1948. Brian-the-Brain couldn't provide the answer – £250 – and Owen left the bank with both arms held high in a victory salute. The question, however, was deemed unfair and inappropriate by Bomber, Connie and the five jar-wielding customers in the bank, who passed their opinion on to the thirty-nine jar-wielding customers still lined up on the footpath. There were several subdued hisses and boos as Owen passed the queue and he was subsequently blacklisted.

By close of business, the bank had received fifty-two jars of small change totalling three hundred and seven dollars and ninety-two cents. Brian had answered two hundred and thirty-two questions and conceded on just eleven, including Owen's. Bomber and Connie had counted five thousand, six hundred and eighty-one coins. These were statistics worthy of Wisden's and deserving of a quiet beer at the Gunner's Arms.

They chose to sneak into the saloon bar for fear of more cricketing questions from the rowdies in the front bar. Bomber stood the round and carried their glasses to one of the small glass-topped tables. Nothing much was said as they took their first sips. Connie and her boss reviewed the weird week that had culminated in their new workmate holding court as the centre of attention while they counted coins. This non-athletic but, at heart, decent young chap was suddenly Mister Popular.

For his part, Brian tried to rationalise the confusion that came from being, for the first time in his life, Mister Popular. Sure, he'd fantasised about it but his fantasies had seen him belting out wailing guitar riffs while screaming young women threw their intimate undergarments onto the stage. Or – like the Beatles' clips – running away from pursuing hordes of screaming young women seeking to rip off his own intimate undergarments.

But here he was, skulking in a saloon bar so as to avoid the rowdies in the front bar. Rowdies whose undergarments didn't hold the slightest interest for him at all. And all because of cricket, which, until a week ago, also hadn't held the slightest interest for him at all. But now, well, it's human nature to pursue those things at which we're successful. A successful portrait painter is unlikely to paint a lot of landscapes, a successful hairdresser is unlikely to file a lot of toenails. People like to build on their successes rather than start from scratch in a new field. It's easier and better for the ego. So, now that Brian had tasted success as a cricket statistician, he found himself taking a more broad-minded interest in cricket in general.

'Y'know,' he said, turning to the boss. 'I could probably help out with the scoring at the game tomorrow. That lady – Joy – didn't seem all that happy to be doing it. If she could show me the ropes, I wouldn't mind filling in for a few hours.'

Bomber smiled over his beer. 'That would be a bloody good idea, Brian. Joy gets a bit spiky at times. She's always a big help around the club but she likes everyone to know that she's…inconvenienced.'

'Joy's got a bloody martyr complex,' added Connie helpfully. 'That's why everyone calls her Joy-less.'

'Well, yes…true…' agreed Bomber. 'But you wouldn't want to voice that opinion within her hearing or you might find yourself becoming the martyr. Anyway,' he turned back to Brian, 'if you can be at the oval around tenish, I'm sure that Joy can introduce you to the pleasures of keeping scores.'

'And then she'll probably complain to everyone that she's being re-placed,' added Connie again, helpfully. She pushed back her chair, 'Right, I'm off for a quick swim. I'll see you both a bit later.'

With all the cricket buzz in the bank over the last couple of days, Brian had nearly forgotten that he'd been invited to the boss's for dinner and a musical jam with Connie and Jillian, the boss's wife. He drained the last of his beer and stood. 'Do you want another, Boss?'

'Nah, thanks, Brian. I'd better push off and give Jillian a hand with the tucker.' He also stood up and, unexpectedly, thrust out his hand. 'You did bloody well this week, young fella. That cricket statistics stunt got everyone talking. Bloody good. See yer in an hour.'

*

Dinner was a barbecue. Bomber – Wal – did the cooking because he was a bloke.

They sat at a cedar-stained pine table on the back veranda. Drifts of onion-infused smoke wafted over them as Jillian laid out glass bowls of potato salad and coleslaw with plates of crusty bread and a collection of sauce bottles.

Eventually, Bomber – Wal – loomed through the blue smoke like a yeti through a snowstorm. Except that this undersized yeti was bald and carrying a platter of snags, patties and prawns. 'Tuck in, all…what you don't eat'll end up being my breakfast.'

It looked like being a lean breakfast for Bomber-Wal, because the barbecue tucker disappeared in short time.

There was a very boozy trifle for dessert but Jillian suggested, 'How about we play a bit of music first? Let the snags settle for a while before we tackle the trifle.'

'Good idea, Jillian,' agreed Connie. 'I'll get the sax from my car.' She raised an eyebrow at Brian. 'Did you bring your guitar?'

'Yep, in the car. I'll get it.'

They set up around the baby grand in the lounge. Jillian unfolded a couple of music stands and Wal carried in kitchen chairs and then uncoiled an extension lead for Brian's amplifier. Under the pretext of tuning, Brian casually ran through a few of his better licks – a bit of Hendrix, a spot of Harrison. Impressive stuff…like he used to play with the Wizards.

Connie assembled her alto sax and Jillian gave her a tuning note from the piano. She made one or two adjustments to the mouthpiece and then ran smoothly through a few arpeggios.

'She's good,' thought Brian and countered with a few bars of Clapton that seemed to draw admiring glances from the ladies.

'What d'you want to start with?' asked Jillian as she flexed fingers and cracked knuckles. She looked to Brian. 'Got any favourites?'

Brian had heard the GeeBees at the 60/40 last weekend. He'd been wondering about this little gathering. What if they wanted to play waltzes and progressive barn dances?

'How about a slow twelve-bar blues just to kick off?' he offered.

'OK,' said the pianist. 'You pick the key and give us a tempo. Connie'll take first solo.'

'OK,' he strummed a few chords. 'In A. Does that suit?'

'Go for it.'

He started a medium-slow beat on the A chord and added the old blues standard 6th and 7th with the little finger. It was really basic stuff but it would give him an indication of how Jillian and Connie would handle some simple blues-rock fundamentals. He'd hit 'em with some fancier stuff later on.

Four bars of A and, as he shifted onto D, he realised that Jillian was playing a walking bass and tinkly little riffs on the piano while Connie was blowing staccato notes on the offbeat. It sounded surprisingly good – smooth, very bluesy.

They ran through the first twelve bars without a hitch and then, on the repeat, Connie let rip with a sax solo so complex, so fluid, that Brian found himself distracted and struggling to keep the beat. It wouldn't have made much difference if he'd stopped playing altogether because Jillian was vamping piano chords in perfect rapport with the sax. He felt the first flicker of doubt. Maybe he'd underestimated these two.

Jillian started the second repeat with a rippling run of triplets from one end of the keyboard to the other and then followed it up with a solo that was just as fluid as the sax. Again, Brian was awestruck to the point of missing the beat. There was barely time for his initial flicker of doubt to flare into certainty before it was his turn to take the solo.

He almost missed his intro but recovered nicely to make it sound like a deliberately syncopated arpeggio although, truth be known, he didn't know a syncopated arpeggio from a buffalo burp. By the fifth bar, he'd fully recovered and was chasing up and down the fretboard like Clapton himself.

And so it went, from one twelve-bar solo to the next. Except that each of Connie's sax solos was different from the last, and each of Jillian's piano solos was different from the last, but each of Brian's guitar solos was pretty much the same as the last one. Finally, after three solos each, Jillian and Connie combined to wrap it up with a standard closing phrase.

Bomber-Wal had been sitting on a settee and keeping beat with his hand against the armrest. He burst into applause. 'Great… Excellent.'

Jillian turned to Connie. 'Top bit of sax there, Connie. You play it like you play netball – tough stuff. Thought I caught a nice bit of Charlie Parker in the second solo.'

Connie smiled. 'Yep, it was. I borrowed a bit of "Dexter Blues". Can't beat old Charlie Parker. And was that a bar or two of the Duke I heard?'

Jillian tinkled a few notes. 'Sure was. And a bit of Joplin.'

They both turned to Brian. 'Nice work, Brian,' said Connie. 'Thought I caught some Hendrix in there. Maybe some Chuck Berry?'

'Chuck Berry?' he thought. 'Nobody plays Chuck Berry.' He nodded and said, 'Thanks.' No denying it; the two ladies had played better than him. This wasn't what he'd been expecting. Nothing like the Gee-Bee's 60/40 crap.

Jillian was riffing through some sheet music. 'One more and then we'll have some dessert. Tell yer what, I found a swing band arrangement for "Choo Choo Ch'Boogie" in a box of old stuff at the church fete. There're keyboard and sax and guitar scores, so it should sound OK. D'yer want to give it a try?'

'Yes, great,' enthused Connie.

'Sure,' said Brian. With all the enthusiasm of someone booking a dental appointment.

Bomber-Wal got up and took the pages from his wife. He passed them on to Connie and Brian while Jillian placed her score on the piano. Connie placed the saxophone score on her music stand. Brian took one look at the guitar score and froze. He only played by ear or by following charts where the score had the chord names written. If it had C written, then he played a C chord. If it had a Bbm7, then he'd go straight to a B-flat-minor-seventh chord, no worries. But this was all black dots. There were various individual black dots for melody passages and clusters of three or four dots which must be chords. He had a rudimentary understanding of music notation – crotchets and quavers and suchlike – but it would take him a week to allocate these black dots to the frets on his fretboard. Shit – none of the Wizards could read music or, if they could, they never let on, because it wasn't cool.

Jillian was already tinkling a few bars and Connie was quietly running through some of the more complicated passages in four flats.

'Er…' began Brian. 'Er…I can't play this.'

'How d'yer mean?' asked Jillian innocently as she continued tinkling. 'Got some tricky bits? We'll try it real slow at first.'

'No. I mean I can't play it. I can't read music.'

Connie looked up. Jillian stopped tinkling. Bomber-Wal sat upright.

Brian felt like he'd just announced 'I've got a highly infectious social disease' or 'I've got a huge boil on my bum.'

There followed a second's silence that lasted about a year.

'Hang on,' queried Connie. 'You mean…you can't read that score?' It was spoken as an inoffensive question with nothing implied or stressed. To Brian's mortified ears it sounded like 'Have you really got a highly infectious social disease with a huge boil on your bum?'

'No,' he replied, abashed. 'I don't have a boi– I mean, I just can't read music…any music.'

'But how did you play that last piece? You sounded pretty good.'

Only pretty good – like Chuck Berry. She didn't say really good. Just pretty good.

He sighed. 'I listen to records and tapes and pick up the music. I mostly play by ear. I can follow chords if they're written down. Like if I see an F written down, then I can hit an F chord straight up. But I can't look at a string of notes and play them like you can.'

'That's amazing,' said Jillian. 'So you can't sight read?' Again, it was a genuine question but it still sounded like an infectious bum-boiler.

'No,' whispered the crestfallen young man. He'd expected to show off some slick licks on his axe – to show these two ladies what real music was all about. The 60/40 had convinced him that music in Gunnery Bay was about twenty years behind the rest of the world. Well, he'd sure got that wrong – the music might be a bit old-hat but the musicians were top-shelf.

It was obvious that Brian was feeling embarrassed.

Jillian tried to find something to lighten the moment. 'Well, you've sure got a feel for that guitar. I've got some scores here with written guitar chords, so we'll give them a go. But, first, I reckon we should break for dessert and a coffee.'

*

The trifle, one of Jillian's many specialities, was superb – layers of custard, fruit and sponge with enough booze to blur the edges. The topping of whipped cream with the Cadbury's Flake stuck into it brought ringing praise. Brian, because he was, at heart, a decent young chap, said all the polite things. But he was, also at heart, a devastated young chap.

Bomber-Wal tried to steer the conversation onto cricket. He recounted Brian's statistical triumphs over Merv and he reminded everyone that Brian had volunteered to do the scoring tomorrow. It worked for a while but trifles don't last forever.

As the last dribble of booze was spooned from the bottom of the tall glass flutes, Jillian prodded the elephant in the room. 'Right, let's try a bit more music.' She led them back into the lounge room and shuffled through more sheet music. 'Here we go, Brian. An oldie but a goody: "Five Foot Two, Eyes of Blue". Do you know it?'

He studied the sheet. There were written chords, so at least he'd be able to strum along. He ran through the first four bars intro: E-flat, D-seventh, D-flat seventh, C-seventh, F-seventh, B-seventh, B-flat seventh. 'I think so.' Then he spotted some weird text. 'Er…what's this "Repeat Good on D.S."?'

'Ah…OK,' said Connie and laid aside her saxophone. She pulled her seat next to Brian. It felt good. 'So, there're two repeat sections and a D.S., that's a *Dal Segno*, and a coda.' She indicated various symbols and text that meant nothing to the guitarist. 'So, we start here, play to this repeat mark and the go back to here. Next time, we skip these bars and go to the repeat bar and play through to here…' And on and on and on…

After walking her finger through the guitar score twice more, she arched her attractive eyebrow at Brian. 'That's it. Reckon you've got it?'

'Yep.' He reckoned that he had. 'Thanks.'

'OK,' said Jillian from the piano. 'Nice and slow first time through. I'll count in four beats and then you and I start the first bar, Brian… you've got two beats of E- flat and two beats of D-seventh.' She demonstrated the timing and the chords on the piano and then counted in the intro.

He started out very tight and mechanical but, after he'd nailed the first repeat passage, he loosened up and got right through to the coda, where he saw something called a *cresc. poco a poco* which Connie hadn't explained, so he botched it.

'Sorry,' he said. But, in fact, he was tickled pink with himself. It was an absolutely crappy piece of music but that didn't matter. What mattered was that he'd pretty well nailed it. He'd kept pace with the ladies and started feeling comfortable with notations that he'd never encountered before.

'Don't be sorry, Brian,' smiled Jillian. 'That was excellent. You had it sorted right from the start.' She looked towards Connie, who nodded. 'Right, let's get it up to speed this time.'

He felt quite pleased with himself when they called it a night at eleven o'clock. Jillian had found two more scores with written guitar chords and, even though the music was rubbish – 'Hello Ma Baby', for heaven's sake – he'd nailed the chords and found that he could add a few little improvisations once he felt comfortable with the basics. He'd learned lots.

It was during a coffee break that he'd learned a bit about the ladies. Jillian had studied piano and voice at the conservatorium. She'd played in lots of bands, backed several big-name touring stars and was a sought-after studio musician. Most recently, before coming to Gunnery Bay, she'd been the assistant accompanist for the state opera company and a private piano teacher.

Connie's CV was also impressive. She'd studied music right up to her final year at a private school in the big smoke, when she scored top marks in both practical and theory. Then she'd been invited to join a youth orchestra for a tour of America. She'd also played in a big-name swing band which toured most of the Australian capitals.

Brian was tempted to ask why two women with such amazing musical credentials could end up playing in a shitty little 60/40 band called the GeeBees in a backwater like Gunnery Bay. He didn't ask, because he was, at heart, a decent young chap. Also he was afraid that such a question might spoil what had turned out to be a real buzz of an evening after a deflating start. Besides, both ladies seemed to be really happy with their lot.

As he packed up his amplifier and guitar, Jillian handed him a wad of folders. 'Not sure if you'd be interested in these, Brian. They're sets of theory notes that I use when I'm teaching. All the basic notations and signatures and symbols and suchlike.' She added a separate file, 'These are all the major and minor scales and arpeggios. I'm not sure how they're played on a guitar fretboard. You can keep them if you like. I've got heaps of copies.'

Connie watched on. 'Wow, Jillian. That must be about a year's worth of lessons.' She turned to Brian. 'Listen, mate, if you can memorise a million years of cricket statistics, you should be able to handle this stuff. If you get stuck on anything, just bring it to work and we can sort it out in our lunch breaks.'

'Learning to read music is the best thing you'll ever do,' added Jillian. 'Once you understand the theory, you'll be able to arrange and write your own stuff. Anyway,' she concluded, 'it's up to you. 'S been a good night and you've got to score the big match tomorrow.' She turned to her husband and, in faux military roar, bawled, 'Wal, chuck these freeloaders out!'

*

Scoring a cricket match was a lot trickier than Brian had imagined. He'd walked to the oval straight after another of the Harridan's ordinary breakfasts of ordinary cereal, ordinary toast and canned jam. He was pretty sure that it was Second World War army surplus plum-and-sawdust jam.

The juniors had just started their match, so he sat with the joyless Joy and learned about the multiple requirements of a scoresheet. Every ball bowled required an entry of some sort. You entered a dot if the ball wasn't scored off – unless it was a bye, which demanded a host of numbers to be added into multiple columns. Whenever a batsman scored even a single run, it had to entered against that batsman's total, the team's total and the bowler's figures for each over, and for his game total. The fall of a wicket – FOW – required both batsman's and team's runs to be totalled and so on and so on…

The joyless Joy was remarkably helpful given that she had to concentrate on every delivery and every stroke. After a while, she gave Brian a scoresheet so that he could practise the required entries. She'd lean over, between overs, to check over his overs against her own overs. Then she'd run through his runs between runs to check that they ran true to her runs – and so on and so on…

The added difficulty came about when people started leaning over Brian's shoulder to check the scores having long since learned never to lean over joyless Joy. Then they had to ask, 'How's it going?'

Brian, struggling to enter every dash, dot and number into the appropriate columns, thought, 'Well, if you can see the score, why do you need to ask how it's going?'

It gradually became apparent that the bigger than usual bunch of spectators had come, not out of interest in a junior cricket match, but out of interest in the new boy – the statistical oracle. For the second time in as many days, Mister Popular felt the gratifying flush that came with being, well, popular. He would have been quite content to have any number of admirers leaning over his shoulder providing they kept their intimate undergarments to themselves.

Joyless Joy, however, was having none of it. It took just a single snapped 'Piss off' to scatter the crowd and leave Brian with a vaguely resentful feeling that his limelight had been dimmed.

*

Hot Gunnery Bay Januaries gave way to stinking Gunnery Bay Februaries. The town fell into a state of listless torpidity.

The frolicking, romping tourists departed, leaving nothing but their cash and smudges of suntan oil flecked with flakes of dried skin. The local kids reclaimed the beach and the jetty for a few precious days before returning to Gunnery Bay area school which, other than the administration office, wasn't air-conditioned. The prefab wooden classrooms each boasted a single ceiling fan which, given that hot air rises, blew hot air down from the ceiling and onto the students' heads, where it got hotter and rose back up to the ceiling fan where it got blown back down onto…and so on and so on. Teachers were too hot to teach and students too hot to learn or misbehave.

In a hundred years, no one has questioned the wisdom of starting the school year in the hottest month of the year. It is one of those traditions invented by someone who neither taught, nor learned nor ever sat in a prefab classroom in somewhere like Gunnery Bay — a tradition perpetuated by bureaucrats who make decisions about schools without ever having worked in one. Sometimes they are transferred to health departments, where they make decisions about hospitals without ever having worked in one of them either. This is called Public Service.

School buses developed vapour locks in the fuel lines and stopped – usually somewhere in the full glare of the sun and exactly midway between the most distant bus stops. Sometimes, after baking in the sun all day, they just didn't start at all and parents had to be summoned in from their farms to pick up their moist, flushed and irritable little cherubs.

The decision to purchase petrol-fuelled buses instead of diesel was made by a Public Service bureaucrat who had not only never worked in a school or a hospital but had never driven a bus either.

Hot, dry northerlies rattled desiccated peppercorn trees against empty corrugated tanks and blighted the town with fine grit. This was the time for bushfires. Sniffing the air for telltale smoke became an almost involuntary action by anyone stepping outside. The regular testing of the Rural Fire Brigade siren at seven o'clock each Monday evening, while expected, still put nerves on edge.

The beach wasn't much help. Sure, the water was refreshing if you could get to it, but the beach sand was about two degrees short of fusing into glass and you could cook snags on the concrete footpath.

Defiance of the rusted 'No Jumping or Diving from Jetty' sign would have been an option but for the fact that the jetty decking was bituminised. The tacky black stuff is really good at sticking to kids' thongs. Many youngsters suddenly found themselves running barefoot on scalding bitumen while their thongs remained firmly stuck three paces back.

The pursuit of a good night's sleep was a Holy Grail. Very few Gunnery Bay bedrooms have air conditioning, other than those little units that fit into half-opened windows and set up harmonic thrums and tinklings with dressing table knick-knacks and loose window latches.

The Harridan didn't believe in air conditioning. 'We didn't have it when I was a girl…' Which was true.

'But,' thought Brian, 'you probably didn't have electricity, carpets or running water in your cave either.'

He bought a small electric fan which he had to smuggle past the Harridan's disapproving scrutiny. It moved the clammy air around a bit but he still woke up hanging half-off the bed with one foot on the lino and the damp sheet stuck to his stomach.

The bank had two little window-mounted air conditioners, one in Bomber's office and one in the window behind Connie's desk. They helped, except that every twenty minutes their drone got out of sequence and set up a harmonic pulsing that set the whole building to vibrating and their ears buzzing. The only way to stop the vibrating and buzzing was to shut one of them off and then start it again. Whenever a customer opened the front door, it would take twenty minutes to cool the blast of February weather laced with the pong of hot bitumen that snuck in with them.

But, despite all of the February discomforts, Brian was a happy lad. His triumphs with cricketing statistics had assuaged, at least partly, the disappointing fact that he was rubbish at actually playing the game. His volunteer cricket scoring had demonstrated that he was, at least, trying to 'fit in'. Bomber Hudson was a good boss and a genuinely good bloke. Brian's three months of training in matters rural had at least given him an understanding of the language, the unique arrangements that existed between banking and farming. It meant that he didn't come across as a total dipstick when he faced customers across the counter.

And Connie: well, Connie was wonderful. She ran the office with the sort of cheerful efficiency that escaped notice because nothing ever went wrong. But it wasn't only as a workmate. She – well, she was encouraging and a confidante and really helpful with the music theory at lunchtimes. Sometimes, Brian struggled to find things that he could ask her about. Sometimes, he already knew the answers but he'd ask her anyway just so he had an excuse to sit with her.

All in all, Brian was starting to feel that he was in front of the game
– he was landing on more ladders than snakes.

*

The cricket final was between the Gunnery Bay Gunners and the Port
Boston Blues. It took place on the Port Boston oval – home of both the
Port Boston Blues and the Port Boston Reds.

Port Boston, about forty kilometres south of Gunnery Bay, was the
regional centre. It was large enough to boast two cricket clubs, each
with as much flair for name-branding as the Gunners. So they boasted
both the inspirationally named Port Boston Reds and the equally inspirationally named Port Boston Blues. They also had two netball clubs
and two football teams. And guess what?

Brian and joyless Joy sat with the Blues scorers in a roped-off section
of the Port Boston oval grandstand. This was serious stuff – not the
place for any casual passers-by to look over a scorer's shoulder and ask,
'How's it going?'

Day one closed with the teams evenly balanced; the Gunners first
innings closed at 212 and the Blues stood at 5 for 141.

Day two saw the Blues dismissed for 212; exactly the same as the
Gunners. Then the Gunners collapsed shortly before tea to be all out
in their second innings for just 92.

Word that the Blues were about to snatch a victory spread throughout Port Boston. By mid-afternoon, the grandstand was full and the
oval was circled by parked cars all facing inwards and all celebrating
every Blues run with a cacophony of horn blasts.

Their celebrations were premature. As so often happens to teams
chasing a low score, the Blues made a mess of things and also collapsed
for just 92, exactly the same as the Gunners. The cricket grand final
was a tie.

Now, more than half of all cricket games end in a draw. This is acceptable to all except those who don't understand the finer points of

91

cricket and can't understand how a game that might go on for two, three, four or five days can end in a draw with everyone quite happy about it.

But a tie – where both teams score identical scores – is both a rarity and memorable.

As the last Blues batsman, having been bowled for zilch, trudged disconsolately from the pitch, the team captains, vice-captains, presidents and secretaries were already gathered in the scorers' roped-off area and scanning the rule book. There they found statutes that gave directions as to what should happen when a grand final is drawn. But nowhere could they find any mention of what should happen in the event of a tie.

Each team put forward their own interpretation of rules that didn't exist and interpretations that would best advantage themselves.

'Countback the season's run totals,' suggested the Blues president, whose monomanic obsession with his team's statistics would see him, in future years, locked away and permanently sedated.

'Play an extra five overs each,' countered the Gunners captain, who reckoned that Johnno's spinners would be unplayable on the deteriorating pitch.

'Replay the entire match,' suggested the coordinator of the Lions Club barbecue, which had sold a million snags and would welcome the opportunity to sell another million.

'Toss a coin,' said the Blues opening pace bowler, who was nursing a crook shoulder.

Tempers began to fray as each idea became more and more ridiculous or more and more outrageously advantageous to one team or the other. Supporters of both teams, now closely packed around the roped-off area, added their own suggestions as to how the impasse might be resolved. Things were on the brink of becoming ugly.

Brian wasn't really in a position to offer a suggestion. He had no authority, no voice. He was only there because he happened to be in the roped-off area. Nevertheless, he spoke up – loudly. It went something like this: 'Oi!…shut…up.'

Surprisingly, they did.

So he went on. 'Why don't we leave it as a tie? There's never been a tie in a grand final before. This could be historic. In ten years' time, no one will remember much about this grand final. But everyone will remember a tie.'

There were a few doubtful nods.

Brian plunged on, 'Does anyone remember any of the scores of the West Indian tour of ten years ago?'

Several people nodded again.

One of them offered, 'Yair…that was the tied test in Brisbane.'

'Right,' smiled Brian. 'But there were five tests in that series. The tied test was the first. Does anyone remember who won the next four?'

No one remembered.

'See,' argued Brian. 'In ten years' time, no one will remember who won and who lost. But leave this game as a tie and people will remember it. We'll all go down in country cricket history. I bet we'll get in the national newspapers.'

Bomber was impressed. He turned to the president of the Blues. 'The lad's right, mate. What we ought to do is get a combined teams photo and whizz it off to the press.'

And that's what they did. The photographer from the *Port Boston Bugle* managed to get both teams with all the club committee members, and the club coaches, and, importantly, the scorers, squeezed into frame. And then they all went off to celebrate a famous victory. A victory with no losers – only winners – at the Port Boston Hotel Motel, which was owned and operated by a local business consortium recently branded, in the fashion of the time, as the PoBoHoMoCo. The hotel's Saturday disco night, which varied from the average weeknight only by dint of loud, canned music, was promoted by a luridly flashing pink assault that strobed PoBoMoHo Disco-auGoGo.

The celebrations were long and loud. Nobody danced – unless blokes embracing other blokes and falling over tables could be described as dancing. Brian was celebrated and embraced as a clever bugger and fell over as many tables as the next bloke.

England won the final test in Sydney, which brought an end to a disappointing series. The elevation of the Chappell boys and the dumping of Bill Lawry had caused a bit of over-the-counter debate but, with the departure of the Poms with the Ashes, interest in cricket waned.

Brian's brain filed away the statistics from the seven-test series for recollection next summer. Then he started to wonder whether it might be a good idea to start collecting football-related statistics in readiness for the forthcoming winter season. It would seem that Brian-the-Brain was assuming a future in Gunnery Bay.

He flew back to the big smoke on two consecutive weekends to play guitar with the Wizards. He'd played with them before and still occasionally spoke on the phone with their bassist, who called himself Stitch.

It was good to get back to playing some real contemporary stuff in real jumping venues but it meant driving to Port Boston, catching the plane, playing till the small hours on Friday and Saturday nights and then catching the return plane flight and then driving back to Gunnery Bay.

By Monday morning, he was totally buggered but, truth be told, happy to be back in Gunnery Bay.

Brian-the-Bloke, meantime, was presenting Brian-the-Brain with reams of music theory taken from Jillian's notes. The scales and arpeggios – just music note progressions displayed as black-dot crotchets on horizontal lines – were no problem for Brian-the-Brain. Just a matter of allocating memory storage space. Working out where those crotchets belonged on a guitar fretboard took a bit longer, because Brian-the-Brain had to tell the fingers of Brian-the-Bloke where to go. This involved eye-brain-hand coordination, which has a sequence. Brian-the-Bloke's eye sees a crotchet sitting on a line. It sends this information to Brian-the-Brain. Brian-the-Brain decides which guitar string, pressed on which fret, would produce the note represented by that crotchet. Brian-the-Brain then decides which of Brian-the-Bloke's fingers would be best placed to press that string against that particular fret. Brian-the-Bloke, acting on Brian-the-Brain's advice, presses the nominated finger on the nominated string against the nominated fret, which then produces the note represented by the crotchet. Brian-the-Brain takes considerable satisfaction from this success and then moves onto the next crotchet.

In this way, Brian worked his way through twelve major scales and twelve minor scales. Each was in both melodic and harmonic form which, truth be told, he didn't really comprehend. It took every February evening in his sweltering bedroom and every lunch break at the bank.

The sweltering evenings in his bedroom weren't much fun, but anything was preferable to watching grainy, blueish ABC television with the Harridan and the co-boarder. Peter Brookman had turned out to be a soppy drip who spent most of his time pining for the girlfriend whom he'd left back in the big smoke. Sometimes, Brian heard him sobbing in his bedroom and figured that the girlfriend was probably better off without the snivelling little wimp. But Brian, because he was, at heart, a decent young chap, said nothing. The Harridan, on the other hand, encouraged Peter's outpourings of melancholy melodrama in the belief that a suffering shared is someone else's suffering enjoyed by herself.

Needless to say that Peter was a big disappointment to Merv Pugnall, the stock manager at Faraday Farming, the double bass player in the GeeBees, the owner of his own collection of Wisden's cricketing almanacs and the recent owner of many jars full of small change.

Brian was aware that his own lack of sporting prowess had, initially at least, been a bit of a disappointment to Bomber. He had, however, gained valuable kudos with his acclaimed cricket statistics tricks, his volunteer scoring and his brilliant suggestion about the grand final tie. By comparison, Peter Brookman was an absolute washout – possibly the most useless transient in the history of Gunnery Bay.

*

Lunch breaks at the bank were a different matter altogether. For starters, it was air-conditioned. Well, yes, the air conditioning was wonderful. But really, for starters, there was Connie.

Connie – she of the short blonde hair who knew a lot about music theory. Connie – she of the short blonde hair and the sky-blue eyes and the tanned, athletic legs and…and who knew a lot about music theory.

Connie was impressed with Brian's progress – musical progress. It was Connie's compliments that kept him slaving over a hot guitar fretboard in his hot bedroom every night. There is nothing quite like a compliment from a beautiful young blonde with athletic legs to keep a young man slaving over his hot fretboard every night.

Brian-the-Brain was voraciously filing away harmonic major scales and melodic minor arpeggios like there was no tomorrow. Brian-the-Bloke, acting on advice from Brian-the-Brain, found his fingers scuttling over his guitar's fretboard like a spider on a barbecue plate. It was an unfamiliar sensation – somehow tingly. It was coordination. Brian-the-Brain and Brian-the-Bloke were, after years of working independently, becoming a single entity – Brian-the-Gestalt.

There were other signs. Not immediately apparent but, on reflection, quite intriguing. He realised that he hadn't stapled his tie to an invoice in over a week nor shut the filing cabinet on his finger. He couldn't remember the last time he'd had to extricate his foot from the wastepaper basket nor clean the sauce off his shirt front after lunch.

Then came a breakthrough, the big moment when Brian-the-Gestalt became so comfortable with himself that he dropped the defining suffixes and became Just-Plain-Brian. It happened in the pub on a Friday.

*

Fridays were a bit of a madhouse at the bank. Bomber kept the place open through the lunch hour so that local businesses could finalise the week's transactions, employees could deposit their pay cheques and customers could withdraw cash for the weekend. This indulgent approach to customer service wasn't sanctioned by head office but Bomber wasn't worried. Bank inspectors never visited the rural branches on Friday, because they liked to get their weekends off to an early start with a boozy Friday lunch back in the big smoke. Bomber's concern for his customers sometimes meant that the staff of NatCom Rural, all three of them, had to work back a bit later than on most weekdays but Bomber always stood a few rounds at the Gunners' Arms afterwards.

The pub had two 8-ball tables, one in the front bar and one in the saloon. You had to put a twenty-cent coin in a slot to get the balls out before you could play a game. The table in the front bar got a bit of a hammering but the one in the saloon was rarely used other than on competition nights.

Bomber would sometimes slip a twenty-cent coin into the slide and the bank staff, all three of them, would casually knock the balls around as they drank beer and discussed society, politics and sport. Brian rarely took up a cue. He'd tried a few shots but never looked like potting a ball.

But on this particular Friday, it was Just-Plain-Brian who took a cue and promptly sank three balls in a row. Bomber looked at Connie. Connie looked at Bomber and they both looked at Just-Plain-Brian. And Just-Plain-Brian looked at the 8-ball table with a shit-did-I-just-do-that? look on his face.

'Do that again,' said Bomber

And Just-Plain-Brian potted another.

'Let's see you pot this one,' said Connie, pointing to the yellow 9-ball hard up against the cushion at the far end of the table.

And Just-Plain-Brian thought about it, walked to the other end to check the angle and then walked back and doubled the yellow 9-ball into the side pocket.

'Bloody hell,' said Connie and Bomber, in unison.

'Shit,' said Just-Plain-Brian with that shit-did-I-just-do-that? look on his face.

'Right,' announced Bomber and slotted in another twenty-cent coin. 'If you're going to be a smart arse, let's at least teach you the rules.'

The Gunners' Arms had two 8-ball teams – predictably Gunners' Arms Red and Gunners' Arms Blue. The Church of England Social Club also had a team, as did the Gunners Lawn Bowls Club, the Gunnery Bay Yacht Club and Butler's Well.

Competitions were on Wednesday nights. Four teams faced off at the pub and two teams played at the yacht club – the only other venue that had two tables. Each team fielded six players: four singles and a doubles pair. It was one of Gunnery Bay's very few mixed-gender pastimes.

Neither Connie nor Bomber belonged to a team but both got an occasional call to fill a vacancy. This was allowed under the local rules of the Gunnery Bay 8-Ball League. Rather than forfeit a match because of player shortage, a team could recruit anyone who happened to be standing around and didn't belong to another team. These emergency stand-ins were called 'ring-ins'. Sometimes a team might need to recruit two or three ring-ins to replace players who might be busy with harvesting or off on holidays or suchlike.

There were other Gunnery Bay 8-ball rules: a ring-in couldn't play on the same team for two consecutive weeks and not more than twice for any team during the twenty-week league season. So, there being six teams, a ring-in could only play in twelve matches during a season.

This rule required some rather strict record-keeping by someone who enjoyed that sort of thing. That someone was Owen Jones – the same Owen Jones who had stumped Brian with an unfair cricket question and been blacklisted for his trouble. Owen was a council clerk who thrived on bureaucracy, procedures and regulations (sections and subsections). His idea of fitting in was to take on the bureaucracy, procedures and regulations (sections and subsections) required of sporting and social clubs and which no one else wanted to do. As a consequence of his willingness, Owen was usually elected, unopposed, to the position of rules secretary of any and every club that he joined. In fact, sometimes Owen found that he'd been elected, unopposed, as rules secretary to clubs even when he'd not agreed to be nominated, nor ever been a member. So Owen Jones's name could be found on the office-holders' rolls of every club from the Gunnery Bay 8-ball League to the Foreshore Beautification Committee. Not because he was popular – quite the opposite. Everyone detested his nitpicking knowledge of constitutional minutiae and his endless points of order. But someone had to undertake these unpopular tasks and Gunnery Bay reckoned that Owen was unlikely to lose many friends because he didn't have any friends to start with.

So it was that, on the following Wednesday night, Owen carefully added Brian Grillitsch to his register of ring-ins under Rule #8, Section #3, Subsection (ii): *Registering substitute player recruit.*

And so it was that, awkwardly, both Connie and Brian were called upon to play ring-in for opposing teams. Connie for Butler's Well and Brian for the Gunners' Arms Blue.

Truth be known, Gunners' Arms Blue had requested that Bomber be their ring-in but he had begged off, claiming a wrist injury, and asked Owen Jones to substitute Brian instead. This was appreciated by all present as a clear case of harmless mischief-making by Bomber.

Connie, as she took a cue and shuffled past Bomber, quietly sidemouthed, 'Sometimes, boss, you can be a proper shit-stirrer.'

'Thank you,' smirked Bomber. 'I'll take that as a compliment.'

A quick review of Rule 6, Section #6, Subsection (vi): *Substitution of substitute player recruit for an alternative substitute player recruit,* one of Owen's favourites (all the sixes in a row), cleared the way for Brian to take up a cue for his maiden game as a ring-in.

A reminder that Rule #14, Section #2, Subsection (vii): *Ranking of a substitute player recruit* stated that a ring-in must be ranked no higher than third on a team's player sheet. This, awkwardly, ensured that Connie and Brian would play against each other in the second game of the night.

Brian won the toss and broke. Connie sunk the 3-red and then narrowly missed sinking the 6-green. Brian doubled the 10-blue into the centre pocket and then followed with the 9-yellow, 11-red, 15-maroon, 13-orange, 12-purple, 14-green and, finally, the 8-black.

He studied the table with his shit-did-I-just-do-that? look. Then he raised his eyes to Connie and mouthed, 'Sorry.'

She shrugged a 'Shit, don't patronise me' shrug and wandered off for a consolatory beer before she had to tackle the Gunners' Arms Blue number three player, Steve 'Roller' Dawe.

Brian's second, and final, game was against the Butler's Well number three player. His name was Len 'Trigger' Reiffel and he managed to sink three balls before Brian cleared the table. He gave the table a 'Shit, I've done it again' look, shook hands with Trigger and wandered off to join Connie and Bomber, who were perched on barstools.

'Well done, lad,' grinned Bomber. 'Two wins out of two. And on 'your debut. You sure that you've never played 8-ball before?

'No,' puzzled Brian. 'I used to have a bit of a go with some of the blokes back home but I couldn't sink a ball to save my life. Half the time I'd bloody near miss the white ball with the cue. Hopeless.'

'Well, you sure picked a fine time to start showing off,' said Connie. She was still smarting slightly from Brian's whitewash in the first game but the consolatory beer was having a soothing effect and, after all, Brian was, at heart, a decent young chap. 'Anyway,' she added. 'I've got to go and play Roller. Let's hope he doesn't start pulling shots out of his backside like you've been doing, Brian.'

After Connie had left for her next game in the saloon bar, Bomber leaned into Brian and spoke conspiratorially over his pint. 'Listen, mate, this 8-ball league can be a bloody good way for you to mix in with the locals. You've already made a good impression with your cricket stats and the scoring…' He glanced around the front bar. Everyone was fixed on the 8-ball game in progress. 'Shit, your idea about the tied cricket final was pure genius. Quick thinking. Bloody good.' He took another swallow. 'I reckon that you're probably fairly crap at actually playing cricket. How about footy? Played much footy?'

'Also crap,' nodded Brian.

'Thought so…you're not exactly built like a footballer. No offence meant.'

'None taken.'

'Good-oh. But it looks like you've really clicked with this 8-ball crowd. Make the most of it, lad.' Another swallow. 'Word of advice: don't join a team. Just keep putting yourself forward as a ring-in. You won't get to play as many games but you'll meet a lot more people from all the clubs. There's churchy types, and the yachties and even the lawn bowlers. A real cross-section of Gunnery Bay.'

Bomber signalled to the barman for two more beers. He slid coins across the bar and continued, 'We get a lot of youngsters in Gunnery Bay…transients. Most of 'em get along OK. 'Specially those that play footy and cricket. Some of 'em become permanents…marry a local. The point is, the good 'uns – the ones that fit in – they're good for business. Your predecessor, Bruce, was a solid defender on the footy field and a more than useful fast bowler. People drifted into the bank every Monday to chat with him…good for customer relations. Connie's the same…good at sport…good for the customers.'

He turned on the bar stool and leaned back with elbows on the bar so that he faced the busy 8-ball table. 'You're crap at footy and cricket – no offence…'

'None taken…so far…'

'He he he, but you're bloody good at that statistics stuff. Customers love it. And now you're bloody good at this 8-ball lark. It's all good for you…and good for the bank. It's a win-win, mate.' The bank manager slid off his stool and drained the last of his beer. 'Right, I'm off. See you in the morning.' He took a step and then stopped and turned. 'Might be a good move to buy Connie a beer. Buy it now and take it through to her in the saloon. Smooth a few ruffled feathers.'

Another step and another hesitation. 'Oh yeah. Don't let on that I said anything…but I heard Jillian and Connie talking about how they might ask you to join the GeeBees once you've nailed the music sight-reading. Keep working on it, mate. It'd be another way of mixing with the locals…especially that good-looking local lass that you just belted at 8-ball. Now, go and buy her that beer.'

*

Brian didn't sleep well that night. A belly full of beer and a head full of thoughts kept him restlessly roaming between his bed and the dunny.

Lying amidst the tangled sheets, he replayed his two 8-ball victories over and over, shot for shot and kept puzzling, 'Shit, did I just do that?' He'd never won anything that involved physical skills other than an egg-and-spoon race when he was six years old. And he'd only won that because the other three competitors had dropped their eggs and no one had noticed the chewy that he'd stuck on the bottom of his egg.

So where had this sudden 8-ball prowess come from?

At around two o'clock in the morning, as he was returning from his fourth tinkle in the dunny, it dawned on him that the many hours of guitar practice had honed his hand-brain-eye coordination. It was this new-found coordination that was occasioning his new-found skill with a cue.

As the day dawned, it also dawned on him that Bomber had thrown a brick-sized hint at him with the suggestion that progress on the guitar would likely lead to progress in other ways.

*

It was a welcome southerly cool change that accompanied the GeeBees out to Butler's Well for the monthly knees-up.

The GeeBees had driven out earlier to get set up. Brian was, again, a passenger in Bomber's Rover 3500.

'Might be the last dance for a while,' announced Bomber as they passed the 'You are leaving Gunnery Bay. Come again' sign. 'The baby's not due for six weeks but the way Jillian's filling out she won't be able to reach the piano.'

This was an uncomfortable topic of conversation for a young single bloke, so Brian tried to steer it sideways. 'She's terrific on the piano. I've been wondering how such a talented musician could…' he started and then tailed off as he realised that this topic could end up being even more uncomfortable.

'…could end up married to a bank manager in Gunnery Bay?' finished Bomber for him. He laughed. 'Well, firstly you have to ask yourself how any woman could resist my endearing charms.' He chuckled again. 'No, Jillian grew up in Port Boston, so she's pretty much a local. She finished high school in the big smoke and then had a few fabulous years chasing her music career…really mixed it with some big names in the game. Then she got homesick and came back to Port Boston for a holiday at the same time that I'd just been appointed assistant manager down there. And we clicked.'

He swung the Rover into a park near the Butler's Well telephone box and turned off the engine. 'She's still got lots of contacts in the music game and gets invitations to fill in for concerts and bands and stuff like that. Nowadays, she's a bit more selective but she flies over to the big smoke a couple of times a year to play piano for some big-name event. She was there for five days just before Christmas. Played piano for the stage band at the Carols by Candlelight in Anzac Park. She loves playing but doesn't like all the bullshit that goes with the music scene, so Gunnery Bay suits her most of the time.'

'How about Connie?' asked Brian, trying to sound casual and disinterested. 'She could really make a name for herself in the music scene.'

Bomber looked sideways at the young man and grinned. 'Connie's a real local…born and bred in Gunnery Bay. Family farm's about ten kilometres out. Like most clever local young 'uns, she went off to finish school in the big smoke. You're right, she could have gone on with her music…got a good start.' He pulled the key out of the dashboard and made to open the car door. 'Then her mum died. Tragic really…got cleaned up by a semi-trailer. Bastard driver was on wake-up pills. Anyway, her dad was getting old and her brother was trying to manage the farm by himself so she chucked it all in and came home.'

Brian had heard Connie mention 'the farm' lots of times but hadn't asked about it. 'So…' he began.

'So she lives out on the farm. Does all the housework out there for her dad and her brother. You've met her brother, 'Singer' Long – real name's Tony. Connie's a terrific kid…worth bottling.' He climbed out of the Rover. 'C'm on, mate. There's dancing and eating to be done.'

*

Brian didn't do any dancing but the trestles were loaded, so he looked forward to doing his fair share of eating. As a newcomer, he'd spent most of his first night at Butler's Well sitting by himself. He felt much more comfortable now that he recognised a lot of bank customers and/or cricket enthusiasts and/or 8-ball players – and they recognised him.

Now, he found himself included in group discussions about cricket, about bushfires and the forthcoming footy season. He noted that the seemingly innocent enquiries from one group of ladies as to 'How are you getting on in Gunnery Bay?' were obviously probing for information about the quality of accommodation at the Harridan's – er, Mrs Harrison's – boarding house. The seemingly innocent questions about '…and do you miss home?' were obviously probing for information about his family situation and, more specifically, about any attachments or special friends that might be waiting, or pining, for his return.

What he found gently amusing was that all the ladies knew that he knew what they were actually asking. They didn't really expect him to spill the beans on either his landlady or his love life but they were experts at judging the skilfulness and tactfulness of his evasions. The ladies came to the conclusion that Brian was, at heart, a decent young chap.

Bomber was greatly amused by the not-so-subtle interrogation by the Gorillas, as he called the ladies. It sounded like a rather offensive sobriquet until he explained that he'd started calling them the Grinning Grillers and it just got shortened to the Gorillas. He'd been put through, and passed, a similar sort of third degree when he'd first taken up his position in Gunnery Bay.

He took advantage of a break in the Gorillas' quizzing to side-mouth mutter, 'You're doing all right, young fellow. Keep sweet with these ladies. They're decent sorts…and good customers.' Then he nodded towards a little group of men and women who sat, close together and straight-backed, in a corner of the hall. There seemed to be an undefined space around them which isolated them from the general sense of well-being that filled the hall. 'Steer clear of those shits,' he hissed.

'Who are they?' asked Brian. 'They look like a bunch of sourpusses.'

'They are. They're the Tuskers,' replied Bomber with a grim smile and a shake of the head.

'Tuskers? So are they all from the one family?' He'd not seen any mention of the Tuskers in the bank's accounts.

'Nah. We call 'em the Tuskers because they're always going "Tsk, tsk, tsk" about something,' explained Bomber, who seemed to have a sobriquet for every group and subgroup in Gunnery Bay. 'They only come to these occasions so they can find something or someone to "Tsk, tsk, tsk" about. They really enjoy a good whinge…bunch of miserable bastards.' He shook his bald head again. 'Never a good word to say about anything…never do anything constructive for the community. Arseholes. Steer clear of 'em.'

Happily, the blokes, other than those who sat with the Tuskers, already had Brian down as, at heart, a decent young chap. True acceptance, however, seemed to involve 'Feel like coming outside for a smoke?' Luckily the first offer was made when Bomber was introducing him to an old farmer with a knotted face and bow legs that you could walk between with an arm full of bamboo. His name was 'the Don'. Not, apparently, Don but 'the Don'. Brian would ask later.

'D'yer feel like coming outside for a smoke?' asked the Don.

'Yair,' replied Bomber. 'OK…thanks.'

Now neither Bomber nor Brian were smokers, so it was a mystery as to why the offer was made – and accepted. Bomber just tipped a wink and they followed the Don outside and over the road to where a crumpled Toyota short-wheelbase Landcruiser was parked in the dark. It was unlocked.

'Hop in,' commanded the Don as he lifted the rear door, pulled out a long-neck beer bottle and, with great dexterity, flicked off the top with his belt buckle.

They hopped in and the Don joined them in the front seat. He took a long pull on the bottle, sighed, wiped the neck and passed it to Bomber. Bomber took a long pull on the bottle, sighed, wiped the neck and passed it to Brian. Brian, quick to catch on to a rhythm, took a long pull on the bottle, sighed, wiped the neck and passed it back to Bomber, who passed it back to the Don, who took a long pull…and so on.

It took four turns across the front seat to empty the long-neck. The Don finished the last drop, burped with intent and dropped the bottle over the back of the seat and onto the floor.

'That's better,' he burped and climbed out of the Toyota without another word.

Bomber and Brian followed him back into the hall, where the Gee-Bees were just launching into a foxtrot. The Don headed for the trestles. Bomber and Brian lagged behind a bit.

'That's something to watch out for, young fella,' side-mouthed his boss. 'This hall is a dry zone. Not officially…just out of deference to the ladies. The blokes who need a beer go out to their cars.'

He nodded towards the old farmer, who was loading up his paper plate like it was going to be his last meal. 'The Don is worth about a million dollars. He does his banking with us but he never comes into the bank. When he wants to do any business, I have to go out to his place. It's a dump. I can never understand these old farts who've got millions but live like pigs.'

The Don left a trail of pickled onions and little cheese cubes as he moved away from the trestles. Bomber and Brian took paper plates and selected a few exotic sandwiches – turkey, cranberry and camembert.

'So does he always take you out to his car for a beer?' asked Brian, who was having a few concerns about the hygiene of sharing a bottle with an old fart who lived like a pig.

'Yair,' grunted Bomber as he carefully checked the contents of another sandwich – possibly metwurst and mustard pickles. 'Him and a lot of other customers. Can't really refuse them. That's why I try to keep on the dance floor – safer to dance with their wives than drink with 'em.' He looked at Brian. 'You'll be getting invited out to the cars now, mate. Rude to refuse. Trick is to look like you're swigging but don't actually drink anything, fake it. If you try to keep up with 'em, you'll end up chundering on your boots.'

He took a square of lemon and coconut slice. Probably Raelene Dunk's – Raelene only ever brought lemon and coconut slice. Her husband of forty years must be sick to the back teeth of lemon and coconut slice.

'Better still,' pondered Bomber, 'you ought to learn to dance…keep in sweet with the ladies. You'd be amazed at how many of these ladies do all of the family finance. The blokes sign the papers but the ladies hold the purse strings.' He took a nibble of lemon and coconut slice, grimaced and surreptitiously tucked it under a lettuce leaf in a bowl of healthy, but untouched, green salad. Metwurst and mustard pickles was safer.

*

Before the dance was over, Brian had been invited out for a smoke six more times. In the interest of good community/bank relations, he accepted every offer. It felt good to know that he was becoming an accepted part of the Gunnery Bay blokes' fraternity. It was also bloody lucky that Bomber had steered him through the bloody ritual and ad-

vised him to fake the bloody swigging. It washn't – er, wasn't – easy but
he tried really hard to only take modderer – er, moderaterater – er, small
– sips.

Even sho – er, so – he was feeling pretty bloody cheerful – bloody
happy, in fact – when Good Old Bomber poured him into his bloody
Rover 35 – er, something – and drove him back to Bunnery – er, Gun-
nery-buddy-Blay.

*

He'd been as quiet as a muddy blouse when he crept in through the
bloody dack bloor at the Harridan's and negotiatiatiated mosht of the
bloody furniture before falling onto his bloody bed.

So he couldn't understand why she was so disapproving with him –
so grumpy and curt – when he finally crawled out of bed to face the
Second World War army surplus plum-and-sawdust jam.

She pushed a tea cup towards him. 'Had a good night then, did
we?'

'Yes. Quite good. Thanks.' Every word was a little stab to the brain.
His eyebrows ached. 'I went to the dance at Butler's Well with the Hudsons. Lots of people there. Good music.'

'By the looks of you, there were a lot of trips out to the cars too.'

'No. Not really.' He took a bite. God, the sawdust-and-plum jam
was awful. And the toast was so – loud. 'I'm just feeling a bit off-colour.
I reckon I've got a bit of a cold coming on.'

'Hrrmmph.' But she poured him another cup of tea. Disapproval
was all very well but boarders were thin on the ground at this time of
the year. And, although she'd never say it openly, he seemed, at heart,
to be a decent young chap.

He went for a walk after breakfast. Along the blustery foreshore and
then out to the end of the jetty and back again. There were only a few
people about – the squally cool change and the risk of being sand-
blasted back to their bones wasn't an inviting proposition. One or two

diehard joggers took their chances, barely making headway against the gusts and barely able to stop when it was up their backsides.

He approached Calibre's Kiosk from downwind. He hadn't been near the place since his second day in Gunnery Bay but, unexpectedly, the salty air now carried strangely enticing suggestions of vinegar and grease. The call of bland fish and limp chips dripping oil and crusted in salt was like a siren's call to a lost mariner – irresistible.

Once again, he sat on the Lions Club wooden bench which looked out to sea. The kiosk and a big pine tree gave him some respite from the gritty wind. This time, there were no holidaymakers frolicking in the crystal-clear green water or romping on the pristine white sands but the same twenty seagulls hung effortlessly in the gale above him and speculated on the possibility of a feed. At least, they looked like the same ones.

The bland fish and limp chips, which just minutes ago had had smelled so tempting, lost their appeal when he opened the oily newspaper wrapping. Once again, it was the sports pages. Brian-the-Brain, despite suffering from Brian-the-Bloke's boozy overindulgence, automatically noted that the Tigers' star recruit had broken down during pre-season training and was likely to miss the first round.

He managed a few nibbles of bland fish but the chips were unpalatable. Every bag of chips should contain a percentage of *morceaux croustillants* – crispy bits – but somehow Calibre's Kiosk made everything as soggy as socks in a puddle.

The seagulls landed. They'd recognised Brian as the, at heart, decent young chap who'd fed them before. He amused himself for a while by tossing chips in high, looping arcs that only the most gymnastic birds could catch in mid-air. Then he tried to help the most intimidated gulls by lobbing chips where the bullies couldn't reach them first. Occasionally, he'd fake a throw and then laugh outright when they looked bemused at not finding the chip that he hadn't thrown. Finally, he created mayhem in the multitude by pitching whole handfuls of little soggy scraps into the middle of the flock.

Then he threw the newspaper wrapping into the Lions Club rubbish bin and was about to head back to the Harridan's when a short, politely British, two-tone car horn announced the presence of a Rover 3500.

Even in its fragile state, Brian-the-Brain figured that the only Rover 3500 within a hundred miles belonged to Bomber Hudson and that the politely British two-tone car horn was probably summoning Just-Plain-Brian.

'Hey, mate.' It was, indeed, Bomber. 'Hop in.'

'G'day, boss,' acknowledged Brian as he slid into the passenger seat. 'How's it going?'

'I'm OK,' smirked Bomber as he selected first gear and pulled smoothly into the non-existent traffic along the Esplanade. 'How about yourself? You were fairly sparking last night…a bit chipper.'

'Yair,' grimaced Brian. 'I didn't get the hang of faking the drinking. Ended up putting away more beer than I thought. I'm not much of a drinker,' he confessed. 'Hope I didn't embarrass myself…or upset anyone.'

'Nah, mate. You weren't too bad. There were plenty of blokes looking a bit more second-hand than you. At least you're a happy drunk. Some blokes get all maudlin or aggressive, or just fall asleep. You just seemed to be a bit bushy-tailed. How'd you wake up?'

'Not too bad…bit of a headache…bit woozy in the guts. Mrs Harrison wasn't too pleased. I thought I'd snuck in pretty quietly last night but apparently I knocked over a bit of furniture in the hallway. She was pretty snotty.'

'Ah,' smiled Bomber. 'Don't worry about Mrs Harrison. She's not happy unless she's got something to whinge about. Just don't make a habit of rolling home pissed too often.'

'I wasn't pissed,' objected Brian. 'Just a bit…sociable. Anyway, I'm all good now.'

'Glad to hear it,' said his boss. 'Actually I was on my way to Mrs Harrison's to pick you up. Then I spotted you feeding the seagulls. I've got instructions from Jillian to fetch you home for lunch. She and Connie were hatching something after the dance last night. I reckon they've got plans for you and your guitar.'

*

Connie was already at the Hudsons' when Bomber and Brian entered the deliciously aromatic kitchen. She and young Carole were playing some sort of peek-a-boo game that had the little girl in stitches. Connie's evident relief at the blokes' arrival suggested that the game, while thrilling for the three-year-old, had been dragging on long enough to become gruelling for the grown-up.

'Here's your dad,' she enthused as she thrust Carole into Bomber's arms. 'Here, Jillian, let me give you a hand with those.' She grabbed a pile of plates before the youngster could resume the peek-a-boo.

Lunch was the full classic Sunday roast: a gigantic wedge of rib-eye beef, a platter of Yorkshire pudding, roast spuds and a bowl of glazed green beans and carrots. Horseradish and mustard pots shared a lazy Susan with a large ceramic gravy boat brimming with, well, gravy.

It was the first traditional roast meal that Brian had enjoyed since his arrival in Gunnery Bay. The Harridan's meals were barely passable in a boiled meat-and-three-veg sort of way. They were probably sustaining and the serves were sizeable-enough in that Brian never left the table hungry for more boiled meat-and-three-veg.

But Jillian's roast was – how to describe it? Sublime? Yes, sublime. The sort of meal that, at once, makes you want to savour each morsel while resisting the urge to wolf it down and beg for seconds. Brian's gastronomic dilemma was resolved with Bomber-Wal's standard invitation to 'Tuck in all. What you don't eat'll end up being my breakfast.'

There was jam roly-poly with custard for dessert and Jillian had decided that this was to be the most opportune time to outline her plan. It was a plan that had Brian as its nucleus, its focus, its *raison d'être*. And, in keeping with the French spin, it also seemed to be a bit of a fait accompli.

111

'So, Brian,' began Jillian as she handed out the steaming sponge desert, 'my advancing condition is making it bloody difficult for me to sit at the piano for more than a few minutes at a time. I'll be OK to do the March gig at Butler's Well but that'll be my last for a while.' She slid a bowl across the table. 'Help yourself to custard. I was the same before Carole was born and for about three months after. So I'm going to be out of action for five or six months and the GeeBees are going to need a replacement…'

'You!' chimed in Connie with an unreadable French expression on her face. Somewhere between *suffisant*, *interrogatoire* and fait accompli.

'*Moi* – er, me?' stammered Brian. In keeping but odd in that he'd failed Year 8 French. 'But I don't play piano.'

'No, but you play a bloody good guitar and I reckon that you've crammed about three years' worth of sight-reading and music theory into the past few weeks.' Her expression changed to one of admiration, which is spelled the same in French. 'I've never seen anybody master so many music concepts in such a short time.'

Brian flushed as red as the jam in his roly-poly. This sort of praise from the delectable Connie was almost enough to challenge the Sunday roast for top spot on his list of Good Things That Have Happened to Me Today. It was an awww shucks moment.

Jillian rescued him. 'We tried a substitute pianist last time,' she explained. 'Bloody disaster. She was a good enough player but just didn't have any feel for the music…didn't sense when to take the melody or when to vamp background for Connie to take the lead. A lot of what we play is sort of spontaneous,' she explained. 'If the dancers are really into a piece of music, then we might extend it with a couple of extra solos or throw in an extra dal segno.'

'Jillian usually makes the call,' added Connie. 'But sometimes Merv or me might give her the nod.'

'So everyone has to be ready to pick up extra solos or suchlike at a moment's notice,' continued Jillian. 'And it's never the same music. One week they'll be right into a military two-step, so we'll extend it. Next time, they'll be looking for a longer foxtrot.'

Wal got up and started clearing the table. Little Carole helped, so it took him twice as long.

'Thing is,' continued Jillian, 'I reckon that I could rejig the piano scores…sort of combine the treble and bass so that you could play chords under Connie's melody lines and take over the melody while she plays long notes underneath. We've had a chat with Digby and Merv. They're both happy with the idea. Digby's a bloody genius when it comes to improvising and Merv can pick some extra solos on double bass. He's bloody good at improvising too. He's also a bit of a fan of yours, Brian. Your trick with the cricket statistics really impressed him.'

Once again, Brian flushed under the onslaught of praise and then he almost combusted when Connie added, 'And Digby was impressed with your antics on the 8-ball table, mate. So they're both dead keen on you joining the GeeBees.'

Brian had grown to really like Merv Pugnall, who was, in many ways, similar to Bomber: a down-to-earth boss who got on well with his rural clients. For his part, Merv had been a bit wary of the young banker until the cricket statistics business, followed by the resolution of the tied final cricket match business, followed by the 8-ball business. Nowadays, when Merv came to NatCom Rural to do business, he was, as often as not, served by young Brian, who seemed to have a good grasp of matters rural. Faraday Farming's most recent young transient, Peter Brookman, had turned out to be a useless drip and Merv couldn't help but to compare him with Brian who had, after an uncertain start, become a real asset to Bomber and the bank.

Brian reckoned that playing with Merv on double bass would be a heap of fun despite the GeeBees' appalling playlist. Unfortunately, Brian's musical accomplishments would probably reinforce Merv's opinion that Peter Brookman, who could include a tin ear amongst his many failings, was indeed a useless drip.

Digby Cole, the drummer, was a different proposition altogether. Where Merv was a large, loud, outgoing, gregarious type, Digby was a slightly built, unsmiling introvert who rarely came out from behind his drum kit. Digby, like Merv, was a customer of NatCom Rural so Brian knew a bit about him. He knew that Digby Cole was Gunnery Bay's only undertaker and that he'd resisted the trend to snappy business names. A pity in a way; Digby Cole's Funeral Services was primed for rebranding as something like Cole's Holes or Dig Me, Digby, or – no, best not. The only time that Digby Cole looked animated, or even alive, was when Jillian gave him the nod for a drum solo. It didn't happen often – military two-steps and waltzes weren't given to drum solos. But flick Digby sixteen bars in the middle of a rock and roll number and he'd go berserk. Getting him to stop at the end of the sixteen bars was the hard part. Let him loose in the middle of a swing number or a bit of jazz and you might as well pack up for the night and leave him to it.

Jillian interrupted his thoughts. 'So I've knocked up four scores for you to try, mate. Fairly simple pieces that you and Connie can work out between you. They're pieces that Digby and Merv only need to fill in background, so you won't need them to rehearse.' She handed him a manilla folder. 'Have a go at these with Connie and let me know how it goes.'

'Bring 'em to work tomorrow,' suggested Connie. 'I'll bring the sax and we can try a run-through over lunch.'

*

March is a month of routine in Gunnery Bay. The new school year is no longer new. Kids get up, catch the bus, come to town, sit through lessons, get on the bus and go home. The daily routines of farming families revolve around meeting the bus twice a day, watering stock, fixing fences and watching the weather.

Pre-season footy training starts around mid-March. It's mostly fitness training, which is fairly boring, so only the dead-keen locals and the keen-to-impress transients turn up for the first few weeks. Truth is, Gunnery Bay sometimes struggles to fill both an A grade and a B grade team, so anybody who turns up is likely to get a game whether they're match-fit or still carrying post-Christmas spare-tyres.

Business in town slows down and just ticks along. Most of the tourist-centred businesses have laid off their casual employees and are staffed by a single family member.

In the midst of all this humdrum, Brian was flat-out like a lizard drinking – busy as a mozzy on a nude beach. Over-the-counter bank business was slow but out-on-the-farm bank business was steady. Bomber took Brian with him on many of his afternoon visits and these were a revelation to the young man.

Some clients were doing it tough – big families with big overdrafts and big overheads. Others were raking it in. Bomber treated them all the same – advising about shifting funds, renegotiating loans or overdrafts, purchasing and selling.

He always introduced Brian as 'Our new bloke from the big smoke… topped his seminar in rural banking…lucky to get him…' And, truth be known, Brian did honestly feel that he was becoming a bit more than just a tag-along. He was coming to grips with the vagaries of life on the land and the special relationships that must be fostered between farmer and banker. So he didn't feel that he was being patronised when Bomber, having offered advice to a client, always turned to his young offsider and, as if to confirm such advice, added, 'What do you think, Brian?'

If spending afternoons with Bomber was interesting, then spending lunchtimes with Connie was just amazing. No sooner had they shut the bank's front door than she'd get out her saxophone or clarinet and he'd haul out his acoustic guitar and they'd start working their way through the GeeBees' music and figuring how best to cover Jillian's piano parts. Sometimes Jillian would waddle through from the bank residence to proffer some more of her arrangements and listen to their duets. Sometimes she'd waddled back wondering if the GeeBees would ever again need her on piano. Connie and Brian had some instinctive musical chemistry happening – and maybe it wasn't just musical?

*

It was decided that they'd try the replacement arrangements at the next Butler's Well dance in March. Jillian would still play piano for a few of the 60% traditional numbers but Connie and Brian would replace the piano with their saxophone and guitar combination for the rest. They'd also play all of the 40% of so-called modern numbers – the music that hardly anyone actually danced to because they were too busy filling their faces at the trestles or out in the cars having a smoke.

This decision called for more practice – more than they could squeeze into their lunch breaks. It was Connie who suggested that they could get several hours of uninterrupted practice out at the Longs' farm. 'And,' she added, 'as long as you're coming out, you might as well come for dinner first. Nothing flash, but it would mean that we'd be able to start rehearsal a bit quicker.'

*

It wasn't flash – a heap of snags and a mountain of mash. A huge bowl of carrots and beans and a bucketful of thick onion gravy came with an invitation to 'Bog in, mate. We don't stand on ceremony around here.' This from 'Singer' Long, Connie's large brother, and Mister – 'Nah, call me Jack' – Long, who was as tall as his son but not as heavily built.

Brian felt immediately comfortable with the two men. Partly, he guessed, because he was there at Connie's invitation and it was obvious that the Longs were a close-knit threesome, and partly because Gunnery Bay had quite quickly recognised that Brian came with Bomber's endorsement – and everyone liked Bomber. Besides, this was a lot better than watery meat-and-three-veg with the Harridan and the Drip.

Dessert was just thick slices of crusty bread and deliciously tangy home-made apricot jam to be washed down with tea while Jack and Singer put Brian through the sort of interrogation befitting the father and brother of an attractive young blonde with athletic legs.

It took twenty intense minutes but he knew that he'd passed muster when Jack pushed the teapot towards him with a 'Pour yourself another, mate.'

116

Connie watched in amusement as her menfolk put her workmate through the wringer. It was done with friendly humour and rather reminiscent of the Butler's Well Gorillas' quizzing with intent.

Finally, she called an end to the cross-examination. 'Right. We've got music to practice, so I reckon you blokes can wash the dishes.' She turned to Brian. 'C'mon, mate. I've set up the spare room for us. Grab your guitar and let's get stuck in.'

*

It was a great night. They practised for about four hours, at the end of which they'd nailed seven modern pieces – three Beatles, a Seekers, one Presley and two generic twelve-bar rock and roll standards that could be slotted into anything from Chubby Checker to Little Richard.

Connie was wonderful – and not only because of her brilliant individual playing. By the end of the session, they were really second-guessing each other – knowing when to take the lead, when to back off a bit, when to follow Jillian's improvised scores and when to spontaneously invent their own. It was breathtaking – which isn't easy for a saxophone player.

As he drove back to Gunnery Bay, Brian felt an exultation; a sense of accomplishment to rival his cricketing statistical triumphs, his grand final resolution and even his 8-ball victories. He'd learned things about music theory and composition that he didn't know existed just a few months ago. He'd found things that could be performed on a guitar that he'd never considered before. He'd come to realise that his dream of becoming a top axeman by aping Eric Clapton & co. was a misguided idea. Copying other people's music was a good way to improve your skills but it wasn't as satisfying as writing your own stuff and, just recently, it was starting to feel a bit dishonest. Every little four-bar riff that he'd injected into Jillian's arrangements had given him the same sort of shit-did-I-just-do-that? satisfaction that came when he'd potted the 8-ball.

And, if that wasn't enough, the little farewell peck on the cheek seemed to somehow accidentally slip around to his mouth and last a fraction of a second longer than your average peck.

*

Monday saw business as usual at NatCom Rural, although Connie seemed to be a bit – distant. Not dismissive or uncivil – just distracted in some way.

At lunchtime, they ran through some of the music that they'd practised on Saturday night. Jillian waddled in with two more arrangements and enthused at their progress although, to Brian at least, it felt a bit flat and lacking in spark. Like most young men when trying to fathom a young lady's unfathomable caprice, he replayed the last few days to discover whether he'd said or done anything inappropriate. He couldn't pinpoint anything but that didn't mean much. Inappropriateness can be quite gender-specific.

At closing time, Connie left without a word as the boss locked up. He gave Brian a quizzically raised eyebrow but only got a buggered-if-I-know shrug in return.

Tuesday passed in much the same way. It was quite warm outside but they didn't need to start the air conditioners because there was already enough chill inside to have penguins reaching for their ugg boots. Come lunchtime and they ran through Jillian's newest arrangements note for note with no added embellishments and little enthusiasm. Brian was getting a bit tetchy – the sort of tetch you get when you can't fathom why someone else is acting tetchy.

Things had thawed a bit by Wednesday, which was just as well because both Brian and Connie were to be ring-ins for the Gunners' Lawn Bowls Club 8-ball team. Apparently, Laurie Porter had slipped a disc at the last 60/40 out at Butler's Well and Irma Trench was in the big smoke for medical reasons, so the Bowlers were two players short.

It transpired that the members of the Gunners' Lawn Bowls Club, who were quite successful when playing on their vast lawn greens, were sadly inept when playing on the vastly smaller greens of the 8-ball tables. They lost convincingly to the Church of England Social Club. Brian and Connie, the ring-ins, were the only Lawn Bowls Club players to each win both of their games. This, apparently, was a new club record – neither Laurie Porter nor Irma Trench had ever won a game. But then neither had any other member of the Gunners' Lawn Bowls Club 8-ball team.

The club captain broke with tradition by buying a second round of port and lemonades for the whole team before they all staggered off into the night leaving the two winning ring-ins sitting together at the bar.

Connie broke the ice. 'Jeeze, two piddling port and lemonades and they're off their heads. Talk about cheap drunks!'

'Yair,' agreed Brian. 'And none of them actually won a game. We were the only ones to win.'

She nodded. They pushed aside their untouched port-and-lemonades and Brian ordered two real beers. Then they sat looking at the bubbles for a while.

'So,' said Connie. She sipped her beer.

'Yep,' he sipped his.

'Butler's Well 60/40 on Saturday.'

'Yep,' another sip.

'We should probably run through the music one more time.'

'Yep.'

'So…do you want to come out to the farm on Friday for a last-minute practice?'

Ah. So maybe he hadn't done or said something inappropriate. Maybe her distraction wasn't his fault. The urge to punch the air and howl with relief was almost irresistible.

He managed to croak, 'Yair. Sounds good. Thanks.'

'OK,' she drained her glass and slid off the bar stool. 'See you tomorrow.'

He watched her go out through the saloon door. Then he waited for a minute. Then he finished his beer, punched the air and howled with relief.

'Everything OK, Brian?' asked Perc the barman.

*

Friday turned out to be momentous. Not in a worldly sense; no wars were declared, no one of any importance was assassinated, no meteor strikes. No, it was momentous in that Brian Grillitsch nearly got skittled at a couple of fate's crossroads.

The day started out normally enough, although the weather was lousy: blustery, cold, gritty and overcast. The sort of day that makes you doubt the advantages of seaside living.

Things were much more bright and sunny inside the bank. Connie was back to her chipper self and Bomber, who always enjoyed the extra hustle and bustle of Fridays, was hustling and bustling between his office and the front counter, where customers were sometimes two deep. The prospect of tomorrow's Butler's Well 60/40 was, for Brian at least, energising and just a bit terrifying, although he was looking forward to that evening's dinner and a last rehearsal out at Connie's place.

There had been a brief lull in the afternoon's business as the locals calculated their weekend fiscal needs. The only customer was the librarian; MrsThelma Pikestaff, who was planning a day in Port Boston with Norma Truscott – she of the raffia lampshades and naughty reading habits. They would probably enjoy a counter lunch at the PoBoHoMo followed by a movie at the Bughouse, which was really the Bostodeon Cinema. Thelma always applied a librarian's thoroughness to her budget and had calculated, to within a ten-cent margin, the cost of a mixed grill, a shandy and a senior's movie ticket. Then she added a dollar as her contribution to Norma's petrol expenses and entered nine dollars and eighty cents on her withdrawal slip.

As Mrs Pikestaff left the bank, Connie sidled up to Brian and side-mouthed in a quizzical voice, 'That mate of yours who calls himself Stitch. He's phoned twice. Says that you need to call him as soon as you can.'

'Ohh? Did he say what it's about?'

'Nope. But he was pretty insistent.'

Bomber was unbending on the bank rules about no personal phone calls.

'OK,' nodded Brian. 'Thanks. I'll call him from the post office after work.'

*

There was no sign of Jack or Singer Long when Brian pulled into the farm driveway two hours later. He would have got there sooner but the phone call to Stitch had taken longer than he'd expected.

Connie met him at the door and took the four long-neck beers that he'd brought with him. She looked great in a tie-dye skirt with frilly peasant blouse and she smelled great in a delicately blended fragrance of evening rose and veal schnitzel.

Still no sign of the Long menfolk as she ushered him into the kitchen-dining room.

'Tony and Dad are off at the Cable Hill field days,' she explained. 'They're thinking of buying a new seed drill.' She checked things on the stove top. 'Grab a seat. Err…maybe pop the top of one of those beers first. Tucker'll be ready in five minutes.'

He took four glasses from the rack over the sink.

'You'll only need two,' she said.

'Right,' he thought. 'Interesting – and potentially awkward.' He poured two beers and took a seat at the table. It was only set for two. 'So, not expecting father or brother for dinner – interesting, and still potentially awkward.'

Dinner was veal schnitzel with mushroom sauce, cheesy potatoes and carrots. It was delicious but not as absorbing as watching her across the table. She ate like an angel and sipped like a siren. Odd – they'd shared many lunches back at the bank but he'd never before noticed her charming chewing or dazzling drinking.

He struggled to keep up his side of the chatter about the bank and the forthcoming 60/40. He'd never before noticed what an enchanting chatterer she was.

As she cleared the table, he realised that he'd never before noticed what a captivating clearer she was. And she was a stunning stacker when it came to piling the dishes on the sink.

'Right,' she said, breaking through his reverie. 'There's orange cake with passionfruit cream for desert but I reckon we should get stuck into a bit of music first. You nip out and grab your guitar and I'll set up the stands.'

*

Their practice was perfect. Once again, they anticipated each other's improvisations and invented solos. They ran through all of Jillian's arrangements and tried a few of tweaks of their own.

After two exciting and productive hours, Connie laid aside her saxophone and turned to Brian. 'I know that I've been a bit moody this week.'

He strummed a C minor. 'A bit.'

She stopped his strumming by laying her hand on his. It felt – tingly.

'Sorry about that…the moodiness, I mean. I just wasn't sure whether to invite you here or not.'

'Ahhh…er…why not?'

'Well…' she paused. 'Well, Dad and Tony are staying over at Cable Hill for the entire weekend. They won't be back until Sunday afternoon.'

'Ahhh…'

'Do you want some orange cake with passionfruit cream now…or later?'

'Ahhh…'

Brian didn't get back to Gunnery Bay that night. They had orange cake with passionfruit cream for breakfast on Saturday.

*

Butler's Well was at its gaudiest best when they arrived at the hall in Brian's car. The telephone box was a beaming beacon and the single strand of coloured lights strung across the front of the hall blazed its incandescent message of welcome to the world. The glaring veranda lights of three houses vied with the two blinding street lights for dazzling dominance. Or it could have been that Connie and Brian were seeing the world as a little more sparkly – a bit more radiantly rose-coloured than it actually was.

In fact, their involvement couldn't have been any more overt if they'd tattooed 'We spent the night together' across their foreheads. And the eye-avoiding, smirking silence from Jillian, Digby and Merv as they set up their instruments couldn't have been any more overt if they'd all tattooed 'Yair, we know' across their foreheads.

At an earlier 60/40 knees-up, several local ladies, the Gorillas, had proven to be adept at interpreting Brian's answers to probing questions like 'any attachments or special friends?' Now those same ladies proved to be particularly proficient at reading body language from across a crowded hall. And the young couple's body language was as easy to read as the first line on an eye chart.

The news – or, better, the gossip – went buzzing through the Butler's Well Hall like bees through a boronia bush. Within minutes, the revelation that Connie and Brian were now involved became the subject of everyone's behind-the-hand mutters. The degree of the involvement was further grist. After all, involvement could mean anything from holding hands to – well, more. The supercilious Tuskers claimed that they had known about it for weeks and didn't approve of holding-hands-before-marriage.

The Harridan was all 'tsk, tsks' and raised eyebrows and huffing and puffing when he tried to sneak in at midday on Sunday. Her radar picked him up as he crept down the passage past the kitchen. Peter Brookman had just sat down to lunch. Over-boiled brisket.

'A moment, Mr Grillitsch,' she rasped as she put down a colander of over-boiled cauliflower and stood, podgy hands on heavy hips, behind the Wimp – the Drip.

Brian was as happy as a budgie in a bran bin. He was in love, he was finding all sorts of ways of being acceptable and his guitar playing was coming along brilliantly. Nothing – not even the flinty glare and sandpaper snarl of Mrs Harrison – could burst his rose-coloured bubble.

He leaned, cross-legged, against the kitchen door frame. All cool and casual. 'Hello, Mrs Harrison. Hi there, Pete.'

'Er…hi,' responded the Wimp as he forked over his greyish brisket. He sensed tension. The crackling bolts of blue lightning arcing across the kitchen table were a bit of a clue even to someone as dense as Peter. He wasn't very good at a lot of things. Reading body language was another of them. You'd need to smack him on the nose with a prosthetic leg before he'd realise that you'd been limping. Otherwise he'd have realised that the Harridan was looking for an explanation for Brian's absence over the weekend and Brian was enjoying the act of not telling her anything.

She, the gossip-sponge, was near to bursting to know what her boarder had been up to. Given half a chance, she'd have Brian strapped to a wooden chair with a lamp glaring in his eyes and electrodes attached to his…to his – person. But that would have been contrary to the code of the widows-who-own-large-and-largely-empty-houses cartel.

Brian just leaned and smiled at his flushing landlady. Then, so as to give the impression that the Harridan was the only person not in-the-know, he winked conspiratorially to his hapless fellow boarder. It was the most – the only – fun he'd had with the Harridan since he'd arrived in Gunnery Bay.

She, steaming, resorted to the we. 'So, we trust that we've had a good weekend?'

Brian nodded happily and looked at Peter. 'Well, we certainly did. How about you, Pete? Did we have a good weekend?'

Peter started to stammer an answer. He'd had a miserable weekend cosseted away in his room writing mushy love letters to his girlfriend. He'd written seven, any one of which would be enough to turn a girl's stomach.

The landlady cut across him. 'It would be good manners, Mr Grillitsch, if we told our landlady when we intended to be absent at mealtimes. It's a crime to waste good food.'

Brian managed to maintain his unfussed, supercilious façade as he stepped from the doorway, placed his palms flat on the kitchen table and leaned forward. He looked at her from across the table, but he spoke down at her from a lofty height. 'You get the same money, Mrs Harrison, whether I'm here for meals or not.' He took the fork from Peter's unresisting grasp. 'As for wasting good food, this…' He picked up a rubbery shred of grey brisket with Peter's fork; it shimmered with congealing fat. '…this isn't good food. This is crap. And…' He hesitated. Should he say the next bit? Yair, what the hell. '…and, I bet Mrs Pikestaff doesn't serve up this sort of rubbish to her boarders.'

There – he'd said it. Maybe a bit harsh but he'd figured that competition between the landlady cartel could be wielded to their boarders' advantage.

He paused for the inevitable outraged intake of breath from the Harridan. He wasn't disappointed and the near-fluorescent flush of crimson that suffused her wobbly face was a bonus.

He continued in the face of her apoplexy. 'And I'd bet that whatever Pete doesn't eat will probably get reheated and dished up for tonight's dinner.'

Another outraged intake, this one accompanied by small, choking noises and the harsh screech of a kitchen chair on lino as she sank onto its seat. Brian figured that he'd better call a ceasefire while he had the advantage and before her heart became as limp as her brisket.

He leaned towards the landlady like a lawyer addressing a hostile witness. 'Good afternoon, Mrs Harrison. And just to be clear, it will be my pleasure to dine here this evening.' He held up the wobbling lump on Pete's fork. 'But I don't want to see this again.'

He turned to Peter, who was eyeing off his plate of flaccid brisket and pliable vegetables with the horrible realisation that he'd seen it before. 'See ya, Pete.'

*

Back in his room, Brian took up his acoustic guitar and strummed his way through a few GeeBees numbers while he pondered. He and Connie had had their first really serious discussion over the orange cake with passionfruit cream. They'd learned a lot – enough to take the involvement to another, albeit uncertain, level.

He started working through Jillian's arrangement of 'Satin Doll', which had some really tricky little duets with the sax, two key changes and some nice chord sequences.

He recalled his pre-Gunnery Bay desire to be a sequin-studded, open-shirted, tight-leathered, spotlight-focused and wealthy guitarist at whom other young men gaped in wonder and young women threw intimate undergarments. He'd admitted it to Connie over breakfast – but not the bit about the undergarments.

As he worked his way through a couple of particularly challenging bars, a silly thought hit him. What if the crowd at the Butler's Well 60/40s started throwing their intimate undergarments?

*

There was no sign of either flaccid brisket or pliable vegetables when Brian took his seat at the Harridan's kitchen table for dinner. There was roast chicken with roast spuds and pumpkin, beans, cauliflower and thick gravy.

Not a word was spoken other than 'Thank you' from the boarders and 'You're welcome' from the landlady as the gravy was passed. A similar exchange occurred as the baked apples and cream appeared for dessert. It wasn't as good as Jillian's roast Sunday lunch but it was a bus ride away from the brisket.

Brian was conciliatory, ultra-polite, gracious and effusive as he rose from the table. 'That was fantastic, Mrs Harrison. Whaddaya reckon, Pete?

'Yair. Fantastic.'

'Hmmmph,' offered the Harridan as she collected the crockery. But there was a bit of a smile within the hmmmph.

The bacon and eggs for breakfast wasn't the only surprise. The Harridan placed two brown paper bags next to their teacups. 'There're chicken and lettuce sandwiches and a couple of home-made chocolate biscuits for your lunch. Don't expect it every day…lunch isn't included with your board. I just used up a bit of leftover chicken.'

'Thanks, Mrs Harrison. That's really nice.'

'Yair,' echoed the Wimp. 'Nice.'

'Yes, well…'

*

The atmosphere in NatCom Rural on Monday morning was a bit fraught. Full of unspoken comments and questioning eyebrows.

Bomber tried to be his usual bouncy, coffee-making self but it felt a bit strained because he was obviously hovering. He affected attention to bank business but he was really just hovering like a kestrel waiting for a short-tailed marsupial gossip to break cover.

Jillian came through from the manager's house at lunchtime to chat, ostensibly, about Saturday's 60/40. She was full of praise for Brian and Connie, which seemed to come out as 'Brian'n'Connie' – one word.

Everyone's conversation reflected the atmosphere – tight, forced, ultra-civil and uncomfortable.

The phone rang and was answered by Connie in her best receptionist-voice. 'NatComRural. Good afternoon. One moment please. I'll just see if he's available.' She held the phone towards Brian and mouthed, 'Stitch.'

Awkward. He lifted an OK-if-I-take-this? eyebrow towards Bomber, who waved an OK in return.

'G'day, Stitch,' he began as Connie, Jillian and Bomber tactfully drifted into the manager's office.

They left the door open.

'Brian, it's on for sure. I just spoke with Thorpe's manager. The Wizards will open the act for Billy Thorpe's tour. Fourteen concerts, mate. Four months on the road. You need to get back here quick, mate. We have to put together a seven-song set.'

'Er…' Brian glanced at the boss's office door, not sure how much they could hear. 'When's it all start happening, Stitch?'

'Like now, mate. Tour starts in two months. Advanced publicity starts in one month. Wizards on the posters and adverts, mate. We'll be made, mate. Made in the shade.'

'Yair, right. What about that guy who's been playing lead…?'

'He's crap, mate. OK for pub gigs but we need you for the tour, mate. Shit, mate…this is Billy Thorpe we're talking about. We have to be top-rate, mate.'

'Yair, right. Couldn't you get someone else to play the –?'

Stitch was wound up. He wasn't listening. 'You can tell the bank to get stuffed, mate. Get out of that dump.'

Tell the bank to get stuffed. Get out of Gunnery Bay. Brian looked at his olive-branch chicken sandwich. Then he looked at the big group photo of the cricket grand final that Bomber had framed and hung next to his office door. Then his gaze drifted down to where his guitar and

Connie's sax leaned seductively against each other behind her desk. 'Sorry, Stitch. You'll have to do it without me.' He hung up.

They must have been listening because he'd no sooner hung up than they all came drifting, nonchalantly, out of Bomber's office.

'Right,' announced the manager in his best bouncy voice. 'Time to open up. I'll get the door.'

This necessitated him stepping back into his office and then out through the door to the customer area. In the brief seconds that he was out of earshot, Connie leaned into Brian. It felt good.

'What did Stitch want?'

'Nothing much. Just some gig that he's got lined up. I told him that I wasn't available.'

Raging

'Right, I'll be off then.' Tom pecked at her cheek and ran the back of his finger down Josh's chubby bare arm. 'Look after your mum.' He winked at her and climbed into the four-wheel drive ute.

She stood on the veranda, Josh heavy on her hip, and watched as the ute crawled down the short gravel driveway towards the little bridge at the bottom of the gully. She couldn't see the bridge now that the bluegums had shot up but she knew from the rattle of hardwood planks and the laboured grinding of the gearbox that she'd get a last glimpse of the ute as it crested the opposite ridge.

Tom knew that she'd still be watching but he still checked in the rear-vision mirror. Then he stuck his arm out of the window and gave half a dozen high, sweeping backhand waves. It was something that he always did.

She turned her face to Josh and blew a raspberry on his cheek. It was something that she always did. 'C'mon, mate. Back to bed for you.'

The early-morning pre-sunrise mist had decided to become a fine drizzle. No surprise there – the forecast was for rain in the afternoon. That's why he'd left early. He'd wanted to get the Brabhams' cattle crush finished so's he could start work on the new pens in the Elliots' shearing shed.

You had to keep a close eye on the weather when you'd got a few jobs on the go. Organise your diary so's you got stuck into the outside jobs when the sun shone and the undercover jobs when it rained. Autumn and winter had been more than usually cold and wet. Good for the farmers but frustrating for Tom. On the rare dry days, he'd be off before sunrise to catch up on the outside work like fencing and fixing roofs and suchlike. He'd been getting a lot of casual work lately. Word had got around that he gave good value for money and did good-quality work – nothing shonky. There was both a good side and a bad side to this. They needed the money to fix up their own place but they also needed the time to do it.

The drizzle had become a bit more persistent. She listened for a moment to the capriccio of water trickling into the new corro tank – part of their self-sufficiency plans. Not that they'd ever stayed here for longer than three or four days. The old place was still a bit primitive. But now, with Tom's growing list of handyman jobs, they might have to think about staying here for longer spells. Didn't make much sense having him driving up from the city and back whenever he had to finish jobs. She wouldn't mind staying longer. Rough and ready it might be but the setting, near the head of a gently sloping valley with its own little creek, was a delight to her.

The bluegum plantation was another part of their self-sufficiency strategy – growing their own firewood at the same time as feeling good about the carbon offset and the wildlife habitat. They'd planted about four hundred tubestock along a stretch of the creek down below the house on the carport side. A month ago, she'd spoken with an enthusiastic bloke from the local landcare group who'd suggested that as they cut firewood they could replace trees with understorey to gradually create a habitat for bandicoots and suchlike.

Now, after only three years, the tops of the bluegums were almost level with the veranda. It felt like she was looking down on a forest canopy and already she'd seen several species of different birds that had taken up residence and a small mob of 'roos often sought shade amongst the trees.

The creek was usually just a trickle with a small waterhole every fifty metres but for the past three weeks it had been running a banker because the Rutherford dam was releasing water from two of its gates. The huge dam was about three kilometres upstream and throughout the year it released what they called an 'environmental flow', which was just enough to keep her creek dribbling and the Rutherford River, on the other side of the ridge, barely flowing. Years ago, there'd been a lot of protests about the dam and the environmental flow was meant to make some sort of restitution. She and Tom hadn't been around back when it had happened but they were grateful that there was always water in their creek. It was named Harris Creek after his great great grandfather. There might be another great in there but it didn't really matter. You'd be hard-pressed to find the creek on any maps.

Anyway, Harris Creek and Rutherford River had been running bankers since the dam had filled up over the wet autumn and winter and they'd had to partially open two of the four gates to release water. She and Tom had driven up there two days ago to have a look at the spectacular frothing overflow. Quite a few locals had gathered there to take photos but you couldn't make conversation because the noise was amazing. The noise and the drizzle had upset Josh, so they hadn't stayed for long. On the drive back, Tom had told her that they'd only had to open all four dam gates once in the past and a lot of places downstream along Rutherford River got badly flooded. Apparently, their house remained high and dry even when Harris Creek burst its banks and their whole valley was inundated. He'd only been a lad at the time and his family had been gathered at the old place for a celebration of some kind. He couldn't remember what. Maybe Grandma's birthday? They'd been stuck there for three days and he reckoned that it was all pretty exciting.

Smiling at the thought of Tom as an excited youngster, she carried her son inside and laid him down in the crib, where he promptly went to sleep. He was good like that – hardly ever made a fuss when she laid him down. Out like a light. Takes after his dad – as soon as he's horizontal, he's snoring. Can't watch TV for five minutes before he's out to it. Comes of working twelve-hour days.

She looked around the room, taking pleasure in its comfortable disarray. They called it the long room because that's what it was: the combination kitchen and dining room and lounge room with the curtained-off bedroom at one end and the ablutions room screened off with plywood at the other. This was the original part of the house, built by Tom's great great grandfather out of hand-quarried sandstone way back in the 1870s. The old quarry was only a short walk up behind the house. They'd wheelbarrowed all of the leftover half-shaped blocks back to the house and she'd used them to build a raised herb garden just in front of the ablutions end of the veranda.

Other than her herb garden and Tom's bolted-on carport, it was much the same now as it had been back then, except that, back then, the three rooms didn't connect. They each had doors that opened onto the full-length bullnosed front veranda. If you wanted to go from the bedroom to the bathroom, you had to walk the length of the veranda, rain or shine, night or day.

One of Tom's first projects was to permanently seal the external doors to the bedroom and the ablutions room and to cut small windows into them to admit more light. From the outside, it still looked much the same as the original frontage but now there was just the single external door from the veranda to the long room. It was flanked by two original small-paned windows and looked, to her eyes at least, a bit like a welcoming face.

One of the next projects on his list was to fix permanent internal walls with doors so that the three rooms would be linked internally. He'd bought all the building materials: permapine, plasterboard, cornices, door frames and suchlike. It was all stacked in one of the back rooms waiting for the time when his days weren't taken up with money-earning handyman jobs.

There were four backrooms, built in pairs over the years as Tom's ancestors proliferated. The first pair, immediately behind the long room and with a short corridor between them, had been home to Tom's great grandfather and great grandmother. The second pair, built behind them on an extension of the corridor, became the living quarters for Tom's grandfather and grandmother.

There were never fewer than two generations living in the house right up until the time when Tom's parents moved to the city, leaving just his grandparents to occupy the rambling place. They'd abandoned the four backrooms and lived in the three front rooms just as she and Tom were doing now.

There was a door between the long room and the corridor that connected the four backrooms but Tom, worried about his valuable handyman tools, had braced and padlocked it. He'd also bolted an old, heavy-duty benchtop across the back door frame at the far end of the corridor so that there was no way into the back rooms other than through the long room. Finally, he'd fitted all of the windows with heavy-duty steel mesh security screens to further deny intruders.

She filled the kettle and switched it on, still marvelling at how much simpler life had become since they'd got the electricity connected. Wouldn't have happened except that their nearest neighbours, Alice and Patrick McCarthy, had started kicking up a stink about how their dairy was always having power blackouts. Got the TV news people interested enough to come out with their cameras and reporters and film a segment about struggling primary producers battling the big power companies.

Everybody who lived near to the McCarthys jumped on the bandwagon. Tom claimed that his construction business was suffering because he couldn't use power tools in his workshop. Truth is, he didn't have a workshop, didn't have a construction business, didn't live permanently in this house and he only used his power tools on his worksites. Nobody contradicted him and nobody checked up on his bullshit. The power company hooked up their place while they were fixing up the McCarthys' place.

They still occasionally used the original old wood stove and, more often, a modern LPG cooker, but now they also enjoyed electric lights, an electric kettle, a microwave and the television. In the evenings, they could switch on the TV news and watch other people kicking up a stink about bastard power companies.

The drizzle had upgraded to light rain. She pulled back the curtains on the window over the sink and peered out. The sky was heavy with blue-black clouds and she heard a grumbling of distant thunder. Tom would be pissed off if he didn't get the Brabhams' cattle crush finished. Maybe she'd give him a call later on and see how he was getting along with it. She'd have to go out onto the corner of the veranda to get a mobile signal, because it never worked indoors. There was some sort of aerial and modem and wifi setup that Tom reckoned would solve their phone problems and get the internet. It was on top of his list of priorities because he needed the phone for his handyman business. Word of mouth had been enough to keep him busy up till now but it wouldn't be enough in the long run.

She'd phone him later when Josh woke up. Meantime, she could get on with her project – her book, *Look a Bit Closer, Lucy*, was almost two-thirds finished. The text was all but complete but she still needed about eight or ten extra full-page colour illustrations and lots of black and white sketches for the beginnings of each chapter.

Lucy, the central character of her book, was her almost-alter-ego. A young lady who combined her visual art skills with her degree in biology, particularly botany and zoology. Well, OK, Lucy was quite a bit younger and didn't have any degrees in natural history. The target readership of this book was the ten- to twelve-year-old demographic and no twelve-year-old would relate to a twenty-six-year-old with a university degree and a baby. So the fictitious Lucy was only fourteen but, despite her youth, she could draw and paint like Julie Vivas and had the curiosity of David Attenborough.

The storyline was a bit shallow. Maybe even a bit girlie. All about the fourteen-year-old Lucy being encouraged by her scientist widower father to 'look a bit closer'. It was, to tell the truth, an excuse to publish about thirty of her watercolour illustrations of Australian plants, and reptiles, and birds and animals.

She'd made a bit of a study of kids' books and come to the conclusion that big, full-page, colour illustrations were the key to success. Parents and grandparents bought illustrated books because they, themselves, enjoyed the illustrations and because a big, colourfully-illustrated book made a more impressive gift than a nothing-but-print novel.

She was, in all modesty, a damn good illustrator. Good enough to have been commissioned to illustrate four kids' books by other authors which, she was certain, had sold because of her pictures and not because of their crappy storylines. Last year, she'd won an industry award for her illustrations and that had been followed by several promising approaches from other authors and publishers.

With Tom's encouragement, she'd taken her full accouchement leave from the university. Twelve months blessed relief from running botany tutorials and workshops. She still had about three months before she had to decide whether she'd return to the uni, or apply for extended leave, or just chuck it in and see how she'd manage as a full-time illustrator and author.

Tom hadn't equivocated. Two weeks after the executor had finalised the paperwork on this place, he'd waltzed into the TAFE office and given notice that he'd be resigning at the end of last year to try his luck as a freelance handyman. He was a damn good teacher but always preferred working with his own hands rather than trying to encourage disinclined yobs to use theirs.

She'd designed and illustrated a slick brochure for Harris the Handyman, featuring a hare wallaby with a tool belt. Well, OK, nobody recognised it as a hare wallaby. Most thought it was a kangaroo. She'd tried to stay with the H alliteration of Harris and handyman but it was hard to find many Australian animals under H other than hair seals, hoary bats or hairy-footed pouch mice. So hare wallaby it was.

They'd visited every neighbour within five kilometres of their place to introduce themselves and leave a brochure. Most neighbours were pleased to invite them in for a cuppa and a chat. As much fact-finding as friendship. A few – only a few – weren't at all welcoming and unlikely to offer work to a newcomer handyman. One surly bloke had actually screwed up their brochure, dropped it at their feet and lurched off to a shed without so much as a grunt. They'd laughed about that and compared him with the sort of archetypical inbred characters portrayed in movies from the Georgia backwoods or the Ozarks. Tom had played a burst of twangy air banjo.

He'd got his first job two days later from Patrick McCarthy, their nearest neighbour and whom they'd met while they were distributing their advertisement. Patrick needed a hand concreting in a row of new posts around his dairy. Since then, they'd become good friends with the McCarthys and Patrick had pointed a fair bit of business Tom's way.

*

The rain didn't seem to be letting up and she could hear more thunder, so she decided not to wait for Josh to wake up before calling Tom to see how he was getting on at the Brabhams'. A flicker of lightning drew her attention to the horizon as she stepped onto the wide veranda. Still a fair way off but the towering blue-black wall of cloud looked particularly ominous. Even as she punched in Tom's number, she could hear the crackling of the electric storm in her phone.

'Hey, Mildred.' He called her Mildred after the American silent movie star Mildred Harris. She who'd married Charlie Chaplin. It was a thing that he always did but only when no one else was listening so he didn't have to be constantly explaining the Harris connection with his hobby of collecting old black and white movie posters.

'Hey, George,' she grinned into the phone. She always called him George – well, truth be known, she used to call him Rolf until the real Rolf Harris became *persona non grata*. She'd changed his nickname to George. It didn't have any obvious Harris connections but it fitted nicely with Mildred as in the late '70s British TV comedy series *George and Mildred*. Her dad had bought her the CD boxed set last Christmas probably to help expunge the inappropriate Rolf from their vocabulary. The old *George and Mildred* series was terribly dated but she still found it, if not laugh-out-loud funny, at least amusing.

'How's it going? Have you seen the storm coming our way?'

'Yeah. Looks impressive, doesn't it?'

'How's the cattle crush? Reckon you'll get it finished today?'

'If the storm holds off for an hour or two, I'll be right. Just got to hang the last gate and then I'm done. I should be –'

A burst of static, sounding like someone shovelling gravel, drowned out his last words and then the phone went dead. She punched in his number again. It rang twice before he answered.

'Shit, that was a bit closer than I thought. Better hang up, Mildred. I'll head over to the Elliotts' after I'm done here.'

Another crackling of static but this time the phone didn't crash.

'Listen, Babe. Can you keep an eye on the creek? It was nearly up to our bridge when I drove over it this morning. If they open the dam gates any more, it might go under. They're supposed to send us a text if they open them any further, but I don't trust them. Give me a call if it gets any higher and I'll come home by the back way.'

'OK. I'll check it out,' she answered. 'Stay dry. And don't stay outside if there's lightning. Love you, George.'

Another hiss and crackle. She heard '…too, Mil…' before she hung up.

Josh was still asleep, so she slowly and quietly pulled up the sides of his cot so's he couldn't climb out or fall out. Then she pulled a plastic poncho over her head and sprinted for the creek.

She thought that she was hearing the wind in the bluegum plantation but when she looked up they were barely moving except to shed the accumulated raindrops from a million leaves. So the fizzing-hissing sound, like a hundred angry possums, had to be coming from the creek.

It was. It was running higher and faster than she'd ever seen it and it was scarier than she'd ever believed it could be. Already the two rows of bluegums nearest to the creek were standing in swirling coffee-coloured water. The approaches to their little bridge were awash and the rushing brown torrent of the creek itself was within millimetres of the planking.

Ordinarily, because she'd never seen their placid little creek look so menacing, she'd have stayed to watch what happened. Nature being dramatic can be very alluring. But, with Josh alone in the house and Tom needing an update on the creek, there was no time for rubber-necking, so she quickly snapped off four photos with her phone and then ran back up the sloping track to the house.

*

Josh was stirring as she removed the poncho and shook off most of the wetness before hanging it over the back of a veranda chair. She gathered him up and found that he was, in one place at least, nearly as damp as she was.

'Hang on, mate. I'll change you in a sec. We need to call Daddy first, OK?'

She dragged a chair to the end of the veranda and, with her squishy son on her lap, pulled out her phone, switched it on and immediately found a text message. 'Warning. Property owners downstream from Rutherford Dam are advised of a significant increase in water release which will result in rising river levels and flow rates. Some minor flood-ing may occur on low-lying areas. For further information please con-tact...' There followed a list of contact phone numbers and online contacts.

'A bit late with the warning,' she grumbled as she brought up Tom's number yet again.

'Hey, Mildred.' She could hear that he was in the car.

'Where are you?'

'Had to give up on the Brabhams'. Too much lightning. Now I'm heading for the Elliotts'. What's up?'

'The creek's nearly over the bridge and it's running really fast. You'll have to use the back way. There's a text warning about the dam. It should be on your phone too.'

'I'll check it after we hang up. Anyway, the back road should be OK. I'll knock off from the Elliotts' early and come home. I just need

139

to do a bit of measuring up so's I can order stuff that I'll need. Should be home in about three hours…maybe four. You and Josh OK?'

'Yeah. We're fine. You just take it easy on the roads. Love you, George.'

'You too, Mildred.'

She'd no sooner hung up than she heard the ping of another incoming text message. 'Probably take him more like five hours,' she thought as she opened the message. The back road, which in one place actually ran in a single lane across the top of the Rutherford Dam wall, would add at least half an hour to his drive home, providing it remained passable. There were a few stretches of gravel that had been washed away once or twice in the past.

'Warning,' she read, 'severe weather warnings for the Rutherford Dam catchment have necessitated further release of water from the storage. Property owners downstream from Rutherford Dam are advised of a significant increase in water release which will result in rising river levels and flow rates. Flooding will occur initially on low-lying areas. For further information please contact…'

So now it wasn't '…minor flooding may occur…' It had been upgraded to 'Flooding will initially occur on low-lying areas…' It wasn't just the revised certainty of flooding, it was the ambiguous addition of 'initially' which suggested that it wasn't only low-lying areas that would become inundated. Suddenly she felt a cold shiver of unsettling doubt. Better phone Tom again and make sure he didn't take any risks trying to get home. Better change Josh's nappy first.

*

With a dry bum Josh now happily amusing himself with a threadbare koala, she turned her attention back to her current illustration: a near-complete study of an adult and two juvenile numbats excavating for termites. It was taped onto a heavy-duty drafting table that they'd got for a song at a government auction. She'd placed the beautiful little animals against a background of tangled boronia, where their striped faces and rumps offered camouflage. Too much camouflage as it had turned out, because now the numbats looked lost against the background. She needed to knock back the contrasts in the boronia with a thin wash of Payne's grey and then bring the numbats forward with some carefully-added highlights in off-white and yellow ochre. This was her favourite part of the illustration process – adding those tiny and carefully considered details that turned a competent representation into an artwork.

They'd positioned her drafting table under a recently improvised skylight. Tom had replaced a small section of the corrugated-iron roof with a metre of clear polycarbonate and then set a glass panel in the matchwood ceiling. The beautiful natural light that usually washed over her artwork was, in a way, quite seductive. She rarely crossed the room without detouring past the table to pass a critical eye over whatever illustration was currently in progress.

Today, however, the natural light was a dull milky grey and not at all enticing, and it seemed to be getting darker. She flicked on the desk lamp clamped to the table's top edge in the hope that, while she wouldn't be able to add the critical highlights to the numbats, she'd at least be able to start knocking back the painting's background. But no, the light simply wasn't good enough for her to accurately judge the subtle tones needed. It wasn't worth taking the chance on ruining an illustration that had accounted for about sixteen hours of her time so far. Reluctantly, she turned off the desk lamp and flipped a protection-sheet over the numbats.

Both Josh and the threadbare koala had drifted off, so she took a cup of tea onto the veranda to watch the developing tempest and see how her husband was getting along.

Now she could see the flicker of lightning strobes reflecting off water at the base of the bluegums. It must have risen by at least a metre in the past half-hour. It would be right over their bridge, so she'd been right to advise Tom. Now it just remained to be seen if the back road was still passable.

The world had grown noticeably gloomier. It wasn't yet midday but it felt like the sun was already setting. There wasn't any horizon. In fact, she couldn't see more than about halfway down their valley. Sharp, noisy squalls were whipping rain across the front of the veranda but, so far, not under it.

It was a world of strobing black and white. Like Tom's old movie posters. 'Should be a crumbling Dracula castle up on that ridge,' she fantasised. 'With a desperate white-nightied heroine pacing the battlements in hope of rescue by a handsome hero.'

Settling back into her favourite wickerwork chair and with her feet up on another, she brought her own hero's number onto the little screen and pressed the call button.

He answered on the second ring. The line, other than brief bursts of static, was remarkably clear. 'Hey, Mildred. I was just going to ring you. How's things looking there?'

'The creek's into the bluegums and there's some strong gusts of wind. It'll soon be as black as a witch's hat here. Looks like it's going to be a real bastard of a storm. Whereabouts are you?'

'Back at the Elliotts. I tried to get home but they've closed the back road. Couldn't even get as far as the dam.'

'Yair, well, you stay there, mate. Don't risk yourself trying to get back here. We'll be OK.'

'Yeah, OK. But they're forecasting heavy rain for at least the next three days, so the dam'll be releasing a lot of water. They're talking about evacuating hundreds of places downstream.'

'Well, I guess if you build on a flood plain you should expect it. We're high and dry here, George. I remember when we first came up here you said that the creek'd have to come up by at least four metres before we got wet feet. You reckoned that it's never come near to that since your great, great-whatever grandfather built it.'

A sudden hiss and crackle drowned out his response. All she heard was '…picked a good spot.'

'Didn't catch that, mate. Lots of static. Look, we'll be OK here for a week if we have to. Plenty of tucker. Got the gas cooker and the wood stove. Got enough clean nappies for three days and I can wash 'em as soon as Josh fills 'em up. You stay at the Elliotts. I'll give you a buzz later this afternoon. Probably have more news by then. Love you, mate.'

'OK. Keep your phone charged up. You could lose the electricity with all this lightning. Get those two kero lamps down from the top of the cupboards and fill 'em up just in case. Love you, Mildred.'

A spattering of freezing raindrops swept under the bullnose veranda like a swarm of Arctic wasps, forcing her to turn away and protect her phone by pressing it against her jumper. 'Bugger this for a joke,' she thought and, abandoning the excitement of the tempest, sought indoor sanctuary.

*

By mid-afternoon the banshee howling of the storm front had passed but dragged in its wake a desultory rain and a drop in temperature. It occurred to her that she'd probably need to light the old wood stove before the long room got too cold for Josh. Probably also need to make up a bed for her and her baby son on the floor in front of the stove.

They'd found an old galvanised washtub when they'd cleaned out one of the back rooms. It would never hold water again but they'd placed it next to the wood stove, where it made a handy container for dry kindling and wood chips. Better bring in a supply of the cut firewood that they'd stacked under the carport before it got too cold. It sounded like she and Josh could be stranded here for a day or two. She felt a ridiculously childish sense of – what? Adventure? Fun? Must be something like Tom had felt when he got stranded here many years ago.

The creek had risen at least another half-metre since she'd last checked. It wasn't a creek any more: it was a proper flood. Every row of bluegums was now inundated and the water level had almost reached the lower limbs of those trees nearest to the house. Maybe about fifty metres from the carport. She guessed that it would have to rise by at least another two metres before it posed any sort of a threat. Tom had once reckoned that if it ever got that high, they'd be building an ark and rounding up two of everything that walked, hopped or slithered.

Below the house and the high ground on which it stood, the brown flood was spreading itself across their valley like boarding-house gravy over stale bread. The steady rain made it impossible to see how far it had gone but she snapped off a couple of phone photos to send to Tom after she'd brought in the firewood.

That done, she opened the flue and front vent, stuffed old newspaper and kindling into the stove's firebox and put a match to it. First the paper, then the thin, dry sticks of kindling and, finally, the wood chips caught alight with a crackling like a chip packet. She sat Josh in his high chair so that he could watch as she fed half a dozen more substantial cut logs into the firebox before damping down the flue and half-closing the vents.

The snap and sputter of burning wood and the bars of warm yellow light radiating from the front vents had the young lad wide-eyed and kicking his chubby little legs with excitement.

'You like that, mate?' She grinned. The warmth felt good on her face. It was amazing how quickly the old stove heated up and how, once it got hot, it would keep the place comfortable right through the night.

She filled their big old cast-iron kettle and heaved it, double-handed, onto the stovetop. Soup and toast for her tonight, and pureed apricot chicken for the lad. All cooked the old-fashioned way. Well, OK, maybe canned tomato vegetable soup and puree out of a jar weren't very old fashioned. But at least the heat was.

In the meantime, she pulled Josh's high chair well back from the stove and gave him a dry biscuit to keep him occupied while she stepped onto the veranda to phone Tom.

'Hey, Mildred. What's happening?' There wasn't any static now that the storm front had passed but there was a lot of echoing noise behind his voice: shouting, engine sounds, clanging and banging.

'What's all that noise? Where are you?'

'Back in Elliotts' shearing shed. They're setting up an emergency centre. Mobile communications caravan, canteen, beds. There's two helicopters outside and trucks everywhere. It's all pretty impressive. They reckon that they'll be evacuating about a thousand people from properties downriver. Hang on…'

A loud thrashing sound, like a mass beating of carpets, replaced his voice before it went silent. She could imagine him pressing his phone to his chest to drown out whatever was making the din.

'Helicopter,' he informed her. 'Geez, they're noisy buggers. Anyway, what's happening back there?'

'The water's about halfway up the bluegums and the whole valley below the house is going under,' she answered. And then, to allay any concerns, added, 'We're high and dry here. Actually, it's all pretty exciting. I've lit the stove and I'm bringing in a heap of wood from the carport.'

'I could get the emergency blokes here to lift you and Josh out in a helicopter if you'd like. Plenty of room to land a chopper up behind the house.'

'No, no, no,' She was adamant. 'They'll need to get those poor buggers evacuated from down the river. We're fine here. Plenty of food and – hang on…' It sounded like another helicopter in the background. Then she realised that it wasn't on his end of the phone. It was right overhead.

The chopper was so close that she could see the features of the observer looking down at her from the square side door. The whumping rotor wash was fearsome; whipping her hair across her face and blowing a typhoon under the veranda. She was forced to turn away from the furore and shield her phone.

Tom heard the uproar and a single 'Shit…'

Maybe the observer in the helicopter had realised that she was being buffeted and told the pilot to move away because the clamorous machine drifted further down the valley. She could now see that the observer has holding some sort of sign with 'OK?' in big block letters.

She tucked her phone into her jacket pocket and gave a double thumbs-up signal and got a cheery wave from the chopper. As it swung round to roar away down the valley, she withdrew the phone and spoke into it.

'You still there?'

'Yeah. What the hell was that?'

'Helicopter nearly blew me off the bloody veranda. S'pose they're checking that we're OK. It's gone now.'

'Yeah. They're drawing up some sort of action plan. Good to know that they know that you're there and that you're OK. Look, I have to go and help these blokes setting up. You go and recharge your phone while you can. Give us another buzz in a couple of hours, OK?'

'Yep, OK. Look after yourself. Love you, George.'

'You too, Mildred.'

It was as she was carrying the third armload of firewood inside that she thought that she'd heard a distant 'Oi!'

*

She hadn't been mistaken. After she dropped her load of firewood, she crept back along the veranda and peeked round the corner, where she could see through the carport and up the track that led past the old quarry and, further on, to the back road up to the dam about three kilometres away.

There was a grey, cut-out figure dimly seen through the rain and still quite a long way off. Far enough that he – she was certain that it was a he – couldn't have seen her while she had been collecting firewood. His unpleasant shout must have been generally directed at the house.

He was heavy-set and seemed to be staggering and slipping on the downward-sloping dirt track as he slowly stumbled his way towards the house. 'Oi!' he repeated every few paces.

It dawned on her that this was the same bloke who'd screwed up

Tom's brochure and dropped it at their feet. He who Tom had likened to one of the yokels from *Deliverance*. One of the pig-squealing, eyes-too-close-together, banjo-plucking inbreds.

They'd since learned that his name was Maurice Pickering, that he was about thirty years old and lived with his aged and near-crippled parents whom no one had seen for years. Patrick McCarthy had advised them that Pickering was '…a sandwich sort of a picnic, a slice short of a loaf, had a kangaroo loose in his top paddock and wasn't the full quid…'

Rumours abounded: Maurice Pickering had spent time in an asylum, in gaol, in a secret sect, in a mental hospital. Tom had estimated that Pickering would have to be about a hundred years old to have spent so much time behind locked doors.

Less amusing was the rumour that he kept his parents under lock and key and the fact that he'd a record of assault. In short, Maurice Pickering was a bloke to steer clear of.

Now that the figure drew closer, she could confirm in her own mind that it was, indeed, Pickering. Hard to mistake that ungainly thickset figure that seemed not to walk as such, but rather to swing one stiff-kneed leg out in front of the other so that he moved in a series of zombie lurches that were emphasised by the slippery downhill track. He wore heavyweight denim trousers and a dark blue jacket – the top half of a suit that he'd bought from an op shop. Patrick had told them that the strange bloke only ever wore industrial-strength denim trousers and op-shop suit jackets over randomly logoed T-shirts.

She took a final fleeting glimpse before scurrying inside, locking the door and shooting the extra top and bottom bolts into place. Then she pulled the curtains across every window. Then she waited.

*

He didn't knock. He slapped the door with a flat hand. Six or seven heavy, insistent and attention-demanding thumps. Had she not been expecting some sort of rapping, she would have been totally startled. Even so, the clamorous strength of Pickering's blows were startling. No point in pretending not to have heard him or of not being at home. The smoke from the wood stove would have been a dead giveaway'

She called up her firmest voice, 'Who is it?'

'Me. Maurice Pickering.' It was a high-pitched, strangled voice like a ripped canvas. And impatient. As if she was expected to know who it was.

'OK,' she thought. 'Keep it calm and reasonable.' 'Hello, Mr Pickering. What can I do for you?'

He was wheezing, breathing hard. 'You can open this bloody door.'

Well, so much for calm and reasonable. 'What do you want, Mr Pickering?'

Another pause for breath. She thought that she heard a muttered 'Fuck' before he raised his voice to a higher-pitched rasp. 'Told you. I want you to open this bloody door.'

'Can't you just tell me why you're here?'

Another 'Fuck', this time more audible and more irritated. 'Because my fucking car's bogged up there and the bloody road's washed away and I can't get home.' Again, the impatient tone suggested that she should have known all this.

'But, but, didn't you know that the road was closed? Didn't anybody tell you?'

'Listen, lady.' He said lady but the sneered tone said, Listen, you dumb bitch. 'The bastards up at the dam put yellow tape across the road. Bastards are always doin' it. Usually doesn't mean anything. I just drove through it. Bastards didn't tell me the bloody road was washed out. You going to let me in?'

Josh had started whimpering. Not surprising. Pickering's voice was straight out of a fearsome fairy tale. Like an evil troll with laryngitis. She picked the frightened baby out of his high chair and rested him on her hip.

'I'm afraid I can't let you in, Mister Pickering. I've no way of helping you to get home. Sorry.'

'Listen, lady,' The gravelly voice becoming more agitated, more threatening and up a pitch, 'I have to use your phone.' Not asking if he could use it. Demanding to use it.

'Well, to hell with you Mr Fucking Pickering,' she thought angrily. 'Phone's not working, Mr Pickering. The tower must have been affected by the flood…' Shit. She'd just told him that she couldn't phone for help. That wasn't real smart. Think, girl: if you can get him away from the house, you could use your phone from the veranda and tell Tom what's happening. 'There's a helicopter on its way to check on everybody. If you go up to the cleared patch up near the quarry and wait, it'll probably be able to help you. Maybe…maybe give you a lift home.'

His response was a hoarse 'That's bullshit, lady' followed by another six violent slaps on the door.

Josh started crying.

'Stop that, Mr Pickering. You're scaring my baby. Just go away.'

'I'll go away,' he panted, 'when I've used the fucking phone, lady.'

'I told you. The phone's not working. Just go and wait for the helicopter.'

'There's…no…bloody…helicopter…lady,' each word punctuated by another hand -slap. 'Don't try to bullshit me. I saw the helicopter heading over to Rutherford River.' His breathing was laboured. This was a very unfit man. It took several seconds before he could continue. 'Probably gone to rescue the stupid bastards who don't know where to build their stupid little farms.'

'My husband's at the Elliotts' place. That's where the emergency centre is. He's sending the helicopter over. He…he…told me just before the phones went out.' It sounded pathetic even as she said it.

'Crap on, lady.' And another series of wild thumps on the door before it suddenly went quiet. Maybe he was leaving?

No, he was trying the other two doors: the doors that once connected the side rooms to the veranda. The doors that Tom had secured to the frames. The doors that still looked like doors but couldn't be forced. She could see Pickering's bullish head silhouette through the little curtained window set into the bedroom door as he tried first the false door handle and then the window's security screen mesh. Each frustrated attempt followed by a barrage of heavy hand slaps and guttural expletives.

She followed his heavy, dragging footsteps along the veranda and saw his dimly silhouetted form cross the two curtained security windows as he moved to the false ablutions door. He seemed to be bent forward and moving with difficulty. Like the hunchback's silhouette in one of Tom's scarier posters.

Another battery of flat-hand slaps as he failed to break in. This had suddenly got really, really scary. She sensed that Pickering's whole focus had moved beyond the need for a telephone. Now he was fixated on getting inside, phone or no phone. It had become a single-minded challenge – a provocation with him. In the back of her mind, she kept hearing Patrick McCarthy's opinion of Pickerin:g '…a sandwich sort of a picnic, a slice short of a loaf, a kangaroo loose in his top paddock and not the full quid…' Patrick had made it sound amusing at the time. Now, on replay, it sounded ominous. The man trying to smash his way inside was obviously off his head – unhinged. God knew what he'd do if he broke in.

Desperately, she thumbed Tom's number onto the phone's screen, hoping against all reason that there might be a signal. There wasn't. Think, girl: you have to get Pickering away from the house so's she could sneak onto the veranda and get a signal.

She heard his struggling gasps as he moved next to the shuttered windows and, when they proved impenetrable, smashed his flat hand against the steel screens and screamed crazily. 'I'm getting in, lady. Like it or not…I'm getting…' His threat was halted by a series of dry, hacking coughs followed by heavy gasping.

A metallic, ratcheting noise had her wondering until she saw, silhouetted through the curtains, his shadowy bulk sliding down the window's steel mesh screens and slowly collapsing onto the veranda.

'Die, you bastard,' she whispered to herself as his wheezing coughs gradually subsided.

But he didn't die. Instead, she heard an animal groan and watched his shadow claw its way back up the security mesh, pause for breath and then leave the veranda.

Moments later came a rattling, clunking crash and a wild scream from the direction of the bedroom window.

'Bastard's fallen over the woodheap in the carport,' she smiled to herself as she crept into the bedroom. 'Hope you break your stupid leg.'

The bedroom's side window looked out into the carport but the makeshift blanket curtain was too heavy for her to see his shadow as he half-heartedly shook the security mesh. 'Bastard's running out of puff,' she thought as he was convulsed with another fit of dry coughing followed by another muttered 'Fuck…'

Two minutes later, she heard him attacking the back door down past the four empty back rooms. His bashing echoed weirdly down the empty corridor but she knew that he'd never get past the bench top that Tom had bolted across the frame. Maybe this was her chance? While he was around the back? Maybe she could sneak onto the veranda?

Josh was crying but she put him down in his cot and offered the thread-bare koala as a comfort. Now that Pickering's frontal attack had quietened, the baby accepted the reassurance.

She slowly and quietly slid the bottom door bolt back and was stretching to the top bolt when, wham! The whole door shook as he threw his full weight against it. She staggered back and let out an involuntary yelp as she fell to the floor. Bastard'd probably enjoy hearing that.

'No one to hear you, lady,' he wheezed. 'I'm getting in there.'

She scrambled on hands and knees to quickly ram the bottom bolt home just before he launched his next full-body slam.

Shit. She'd heard some sort of splintering sound with that last assault. How much more would the door take? She eased open a tiny crack in the window curtains and risked a peek. He was standing – no, leaning – against a veranda post and massaging a shoulder. Shit, but he was a big bloke. But fat and unhealthy-looking. Sure, he was thickset and probably quite powerful if he got you in his grip but he didn't look like a man who was used to hard work and they'd seen that his farm was a run-down dump that looked like no one had ever done a stick of work on the place. And now also nursing a sore shoulder. So much the better.

He must have noticed the slight flicker of the curtain as she closed the gap. Pushing himself away from the veranda post, he lurched the four paces to the window to smack both hands against the mesh. His hysterical 'Open it, you bitch. Open it,' was more a high-pitched grating whisper than scream. An animal in pain. He staggered back to the support of the veranda post, where he doubled-up in another spasm of coughing.

His next attack on the front door wasn't as violent but she definitely heard that faint but unnerving splintering sound again. Something was giving way.

'Stop it, you stupid bastard,' she screamed.

From his crib, Josh joined in.

She felt herself trembling and hated herself for it. 'To hell with this. The bastard's got us both scared.' A few deep breaths to take the tremor out of her voice and then, in a higher scream, 'I've got a gun in here, Pickering. You step one foot in here and I'll blow your stupid head off.'

A moment's pause. He was thinking about that. Then, in a voice dripping with croaking scorn, 'Yeah, lady. Sure you have. Firstly you haven't got a phone and now you've got a gun. Bullshit, lady.'

'You set one foot in here, you bastard and –'

'Yeah, yeah, you already said that, lady.' She could sense his malevolent smile. 'What sort of gun've you got in there, lady? A machine gun?'

'It's…it's…a shotgun.' Bugger, that sounded weak. Again, stronger, 'A shotgun, Pickering. A bloody shotgun.'

'Oh? A shotgun? Geez, lady. A shotgun. Sounds really scary. Do you even know what a shotgun looks like, lady? You'd probably blow your own fucking head off with a real shotgun.'

She could hear from his heavy breathing that he was leaning against the door as he spoke. She dared to press her face against it, just millimetres from him, and screamed, 'Don't kid yourself, you fucking arsehole. I know how to use it.'

The sudden closeness of her voice must have come as a shock. He took a single staggered step backwards before gathering himself and replying in a mocking sing-song, 'Scary, scary, scary. Lady got a shotgun. Scary, scary, scary.'

He threw himself at the door again but definitely with less force. She heard a muttered 'Faaarr' and several loud gasps which she took to mean that he'd hurt himself again. Good. Maybe he'd stop body-slamming the door.

Those faint splintering sounds had her really worried, so she ran her eyes and hands around the door frame and the bolts, looking for any signs of weakness – any signs that his attacks were having effect. Nothing obvious; no loosened screws, no splinters. The nine-inch-thick hardwood frame bolted to the two-foot-thick stone walls seemed to have the heavy-duty braced door firmly in their grasp. So, hopefully, the splintering sounds didn't mean anything.

'Scary, scary, scary. Lady got a shotgun. Scary, scary, scary.' This time his whiny and ragged schoolyard chant was accompanied by slightly off-beat hand slaps on the door.

So was this meant to be psychological warfare now? Did he really think that she'd surrender in the face of his shithouse singing and dopey lyrics? A hundred responsive goads offered themselves to her but she bit them back. No point aggravating the stupid moron any more than he already was.

Instead, she picked up Josh, walked him quietly around the room while she hummed an accompaniment to Pickering's taunt. Turning his crappy chant into a lullaby. The childish tune, like one of those young girls' skipping chants, wasn't difficult to pick up and it gave both her and her baby a bit of comfort.

She hadn't noticed how dark the room had become. The only light, now that the curtains were drawn, came from the skylight. She wouldn't turn on the electric lights because that would reveal any chinks in the curtains to Pickering. Maybe show him where he might be able to see inside.

'Scary, scary, scary. Lady got a shotgun. Scary, scary, scary.'

'Scary, scary, scary. Lady got a shotgun. Scary, scary, scary.'

'Scary, scary, scary. Lady got a shotgun. Scary, scary, scary.'

'Scary, scary, scary. Lady got…' His chant became a burst of racking cough and choking for breath.

He tried another verse but only got as far as 'Scary, scary' before he broke down in a spasm of croaks. Then, gasping, he left the veranda.

And then things went quiet.

Josh had drifted off, so she stopped crooning and dared to peek through the curtains again. No sign of him and no sound. She found the bastard's silence to be more unnerving than his rampages or his singing. At least she knew where he was when he was thumping the doors or chanting. But then, maybe he was in worse condition than she'd thought. Maybe throwing himself against doors was taking a bigger toll than she'd hoped. Maybe the bastard was having a heart attack.

She laid Josh and the threadbare koala back in his crib before quietly and carefully doing the rounds of the windows. Easing each of the curtains open by just a crack so that she could see where he was and what condition he was in. Nothing – not on the veranda and not under the carport. So he had to be around the back somewhere. Probably behind the four back rooms. No way of checking and she wasn't about to risk unbolting and opening the door between the long room and the back corridor. Besides, he'd got nowhere when he'd tried the back door, which had the added security of Tom's bolted-over benchtop.

Then she became aware of an ominous scraping and creaking that seemed to be coming from somewhere down in the back rooms. Shit. Surely the bastard hadn't managed to get past the bolted back door. Christ. You'd need dynamite to get through it. There wasn't anything back there that he could have used to lever it off. Tom was fanatical about keeping all the tools locked up indoors. She ran an inventory through her mind: spades, rakes, axes. No, there was nothing left out back…except…except, maybe the old wooden ladder. The old wooden ladder that they'd used to clean out the gutters, but he couldn't have used that to lever open the door.

But, hang on, he could use it to get onto the roof. That was the lowest part of the roof back there where it sloped right down over the four back rooms. But it was a rickety old wooden ladder that surely wouldn't hold Pickering's clumsy weight. Would it?

There. Another creaking sound. Like floorboards complaining. Like a coffin lid opening. Was he creeping up the corridor? If he got to the door that separated the corridor from the long room, would it keep him out? Tom had fixed two extra bolts but it wasn't as robust as the exterior front door. At least it was built to open outwards – into the corridor. So if he tried to shoulder it open, he'd be pushing against the door jamb.

Was there anything that she could jam against the door? Her drafting table maybe? It was bloody heavy enough when they'd manoeuvred it in here. Shoving with all of her weight shifted it by about three centimetres and left her panting. The door was about two metres away. Shit. It'd take her a bloody week to move it that far.

A dull thump followed by an odd metallic scrambling sound had her momentarily puzzled. Then it dawned on her. He'd slipped and fallen. So, not in the corridor. He was on the roof. Somehow he'd managed to use that bloody ladder. 'Geez,' she thought aloud. 'The dickhead's half crippled, and he's overweight, and he's already hurt himself trying to smash through the door. It's his bloody stupid obsession that's driving him. The man's off his nut. He's demented.'

It was still raining, so it'd be bloody slippery up there although the slope over the back rooms wasn't very steep. The gable roof over the original part of the house was a lot steeper. But why was he on the roof? Was he so far beyond logic, beyond reason, that he thought that he'd find a way inside through the roof? What did he think he could do? Rip off the corro with his teeth?

What about the skylight? Was that clear polycarbonate panel strong enough to hold Pickering's weight? He'd have to climb up the rear slope of the original gable roof and over the ridge cap to get to it. Right over her drafting table. Right over her numbats.

As she rolled Josh's crib out of the long room and into their bedroom, she heard more scrambling. No doubt about it, he was trying to climb up the steeper slope. So he'd managed to get across the easy slope of the skillion roof over the four back rooms and now he was over the long room.

It wasn't difficult to picture Pickering's movements. She'd been able to track Tom when he had worked on the roof and he was a lot lighter and more nimble than the big, fat, deranged lump who was scrabbling to get up the steep slope to the ridge cap. It was almost comical to hear his boots trying to get a grip, and then a dull thud and grating as he lost purchase and slid back down. He must be hurting like hell and as wet as a shag. He must be stone-cold crazy.

Time and again, she heard him fail until, at last, the scratching-scrambling stopped and it sounded as if he'd given up and was making his way back over the flat skillion roof to the ladder. But no – he was getting a run-up. Somehow the corrugated roof didn't buckle under the five massively heavy footfalls before he threw himself up towards the highest point – the ridge cap. She actually saw the ceiling shudder and was sure that he was about to come crashing through but, after a series of frantic clawings, he pulled himself onto and astride the ridge cap.

She became aware that her whole body was trembling and that she was staring at the ceiling. She and Tom had sat up there, back when he was working on the skylight. He'd helped her up onto the roof and they'd sat there, pointing out landmarks, jokingly tracing the boundaries of their newly -inherited Harris Estate and tracing the tree-lined course of Harris Creek right down to the far end of their valley. Somewhere beyond the valley, it eventually spilled into Rutherford River.

It came as a flush of red-hot rage to visualise Pickering – that fat, fucking, psychopathic gargoyle – sitting up there on their perch. Nah – she wasn't having that.

He moved. She heard several short, skipping shuffles and imagined the bastard carefully working his way down the steep slope towards the front of the house. He'd be right over the skylight in a moment.

Yair – there he was. She could see that he was bending over, trying to see into the long room. She knew that the corrugated polycarbonate panel made it impossible to see through but his bulk blocked out the light like the shadow of doom.

The roof was sound. Tom had checked the timbers and reinforced those few joists that needed strengthening but, even so, Pickering's un-balanced weight was causing some ominous creaking. Several sharp thuds told her that he was testing the polycarb with his boot. They weren't really heavy thuds. She guessed that he probably wasn't able to bring his full weight down because the slope of the roof would make it very hard to balance on one leg. But if he stepped onto the clear sheet, he'd probably come crashing straight through it. And through the ceil-ing. And into the long room.

OK. The bastard's up there. Now's the time to get outside and onto the veranda. Where the phone would work.

'Yoo-hoo, lady. Looks like I found a way in. Looks like…'

She didn't hear the rest of his taunt as she ripped back the door bolts and stepped outside. Then, almost as an afterthought, she reached back and flipped on all of the interior lights. But not the veranda light. She wasn't carrying her phone – she had something better.

The rain had moderated to nothing more than a light drizzle but she was still dripping by the time she'd taken half a dozen steps out from under the shelter of the veranda and turned towards the house. The light spilling from the opened front door threw a sharply defined yellow rectangle across the veranda and onto the sparkling wet grass. She moved out of the light and stood in the shadow – to where Picker-ing wouldn't immediately see her.

The sky was a lowering, grumbling blue-black cyclorama shot through with lightning flares. Pickering was on the roof, bent over the skylight, still yelling and not aware that she was below. Watching him.

The thick, clumsy and hunched figure, now dramatically underlit by the skylight was straight out of Tom's black and white poster collection. Lon Chaney in *The Hunchback* or *The Phantom*. Striking but horrible images that she'd forbidden him from hanging on the walls lest they scare Josh.

'Oi!' She screamed. 'Arsehole!'

He straightened, and the light from beneath raced up his contorted figure to wash across his face but leaving his eyes as hideous, dark sockets. For a moment, as he adjusted from the glare of the skylight to the gloom, he twisted, searching for the voice and almost staggering on the sloping corrugated roof.

'Down here. Arsehole!'

Shielding his eyes from the underlight, he took a sliding step forward. Now he was a black shape against a gunmetal background. She took a single sideways step into the light.

'Well, well. The lady has got a shotgun after all. Careful you don't knock yourself over, lady. Those things can be…'

He didn't finish his warning. She braced the Beretta over-and-under shotgun against her shoulder and fired. Later, as she replayed the scene in her mind, she'd realise that she was always going to shoot him. Never in doubt. No second thoughts. No second chances. No choice.

It was one of her older guns. Not one that she used in competition clay shoots. Not the one that she'd used to win the last state championship. This old twelve-gauge Beretta had the thirty-inch barrel with the choke designed for a tighter pattern of shot. She'd loaded it with low-power shells and number nine steel shot. Enough to powder a clay pigeon but not much more.

Usually, of course, she'd be aiming at a moving clay target as it tracked across her field of vision twenty metres away. So it wasn't a difficult challenge to hit Pickering's stationary left knee at a range of about fifteen metres.

He bellowed and staggered as his left knee buckled with the impact. He clutched at the pain but the pitched roof forced him to take four lurching steps downward and onto the bull-nosed corrugations of the veranda.

His impetus sent him staggering across the veranda roof until his foot caught in the guttering and flipped him, headfirst, down and onto her herb garden – the herb garden that she and Tom had constructed from leftover stones from the old quarry. His death dance, from the skylight to the herb garden, had taken the last eight seconds of his life.

She studied the inert body for another eight seconds before breaking open the shotgun and retrieving the single spent shell for reloading later. 'Bugger,' she muttered. Then she went back inside to carefully wipe down the gun and use a pull-through to clean the gunpowder smell from the bore. Then she wheeled Josh's crib back into the long room, fed him another biscuit and fed two more logs into the wood stove.

*

None of the number nine shot had penetrated his thick denim trousers and, being steel, there wouldn't be any tell-tale lead residue. Even so, she was painstaking in her examination of his body for any sign that might suggest that he'd been shot. This was important because, first off, it was against the law to shoot anybody. Sure, she'd almost certainly get away with a plea of self-defence. Trouble was, the shotgun that she'd used was meant to be securely locked away back home in the big smoke and not up here in their temporary residence where she'd thought that she might get in a bit of practice. She could lose her gun licence and probably be banned from competition.

There would surely be some sort of enquiry when they found his body. She ran through a few scenarios as she checked for steel shot in the weave of his denim trousers. The caved-in head wound that had killed him wouldn't be a problem. Put it down as an accident that caused him to fall into the flood. Same with the bruised knee. Must have happened when he'd abandoned his bogged car and tried to walk home. Should have known better. No, sorry – she hadn't seen or heard anything. Been inside with Josh most of the time. The storm had been really loud and scary. No, nobody had come near the place since the helicopter had checked up on her. Maybe the blokes in the chopper had seen something? No? Well, there you go then. Sorry to hear that the poor bugger had drowned, We'd only met him once, didn't seem to be very fit, not very steady on his feet.'

*

The rain was easing but, nevertheless, she slipped a bit as she rolled the bulky body down the slope and into the frothing torrent. She was a bit pissed off when he got stuck and she got water in her boots trying to push him out further.

She watched as he drifted away, rotating slowly in the current. Quite sedate in a way. If he didn't get snagged on anything, he could drift into Rutherford River by morning.

Careful of the treacherously slippery wet grass, she trudged back up to the house and set her boots to dry in front of the stove. She checked Josh and the threadbare koala. They were both peacefully asleep, so she took her mobile out onto the veranda, settled herself into the wicker chair and punched in Tom's number'

He answered after six rings. 'Hey, Mildred.'

'Hey, George.' She listened for a moment before answering. 'No, we're fine, George. Everything's calm. We've got moon and stars over-head now.'

A pause while she listened. 'No, nowhere near us. It's running pretty fast but it's not got any higher. Too dark to see anything until tomorrow but we're high and dry. Just the two of us on our own little island.'

Another pause. 'Josh is fine. We'll sleep on the mattress near the wood stove. He loves it when we do that. OK, George, I'll buzz you in the morning. Love you, George.'

She rang off, went back indoors to the warmth. As she stepped past the drafting table, she flipped back the cover sheet. It was a bloody good illustration. She'd get it finished tomorrow. No worries.

A Teller of Tales

I first met Allman Semper in the Hero of Waterloo Hotel in May of 1872. When I say 'first met', I should probably say 'first overheard', for he was sitting with a handsome couple in the dining room where I sat, by myself and with my back towards them, at an adjacent table. I'd briefly nodded to them as I'd been shown to my lonely table and I'd been left with the impression of a well-to-do, fashionably dressed couple facing a lean and clean-shaven fellow whose lounge suit, of somewhat coarser fabric than that of his companions, could best be described as utilitarian.

Not that I was in a position to criticise another's suit. My own travel-creased morning coat and disarranged four-in-hand declared to the world that this agricultural hardware salesman didn't invest much of his modest income on quality tailoring.

I was in Sydney to peddle fencing materials at the State Agricultural Show. Nothing extraordinary – just staples, pickets, gates in various widths, wire in three gauges and an assortment of fencing tools. Despite the mundane nature of my wares, I'd had a good few days and written many orders. I was feeling content with myself and believed that old Throsby – he who owned the company for which I worked – would grudgingly appreciate my efforts.

The agricultural show had drawn thousands through the gates. Mostly city types who still thought of themselves as connected to the bush but who wouldn't know a strainer post from a sheep dip. The men usually gathered around the gaudy stalls displaying the latest in water pumps and soil-tilling devices while their wives were inveigled by demonstrations of crafts and sewing machines.

My success lay in the fact that not everyone needs new ploughs or mangles but nearly everyone, not just farmers and graziers, would regularly need new fencing materials. The orders for the range of Throsby decorative garden gates, for example, filled half a book.

As I dined, I found myself becoming rather annoyed with the intrusion of Semper's insistent voice into my own thoughts. Not only because I was trying to write an inspirational account of my day but because I only caught tantalising snippets of what sounded like an enthralling story.

I'm a writer – well, I like to write whenever I'm not engaged in selling hardware. Often it amounts to nothing more than a recount of the day's doings which, when one spends most days wrestling with fencing wire, doesn't result in an enthralling read. But I've had an occasional short story published in the *Mallee Mail* and Mr Throsby relies on me to compose his company's brochures and advertisements.

Then there was my novel, which was still without a name and, truth be told, without a properly constructed plot. I had a hero – a young lad who'd escaped from a tyrannical stepfather to become a riverboat skipper out of Echuca. A resourceful lad, Ralf Gordon owed his Christian name to James Tucker's novel and his surname to Adam Lindsay. I'd determined that, somehow, he'd perform heroic deeds and ultimately make his fortune on the river. I'd concocted several potentially heroic deeds but how he was to make his fortune had been, up till now, undetermined.

I say up till now because I'd had a few fortune-making notions between writing orders for crowbars and strainers. I'd thought that young Ralf Gordon might gather together all of the newfangled agricultural and domestic devices on display and load them onto his riverboat, which would then become transformed into a travelling agricultural show. The purveyors of the devices would pay him a substantial commission to participate in his extravaganza. In my imagination, Ralf Gordon's riverboat spectacular would make London's Crystal Palace Exhibition of 1851 look like a sideshow carnival.

So it was into my unfolding idea, my grandiose conceptualisation, that the fragments of Allman Semper's storytelling intruded. Torn between writing my own story and listening to his, I wolfed down my jam pudding with lumpy custard and retreated to my room. There, undistracted, I scribbled four pages of exhilarating headway in the saga of Ralf Gordon.

*

I was surprised to find Allman Semper sitting at the same dining room table but with a different well-to-do couple when, on the following evening, I was again shown to my single seat. The storyteller was holding the husband and wife in open-mouthed thrall and didn't break the flow of his narrative as we acknowledged each other with a brief nod.

I had nothing to add to my diary. Sales at the agricultural show had been steady and I'd fleshed out the skeleton of Ralf Gordon's riverboat exhibition between writing orders for gates and hinges. So, other than a rather good porterhouse steak, I had nothing on which to concentrate but Semper's story. I soon had no doubts that it was the same tale being retold – a gripping story about a young medical orderly at the Battle of Waterloo. My first thought was that there must be some association between Semper's story and the venue – The Hero of Waterloo Hotel – because, when it came to pursuing a theme, this pub was more obsessed with the Duke of Wellington than had been all of England sixty years earlier. An heroic depiction of the duke astride a rearing battle horse hung above the entrance and the dining room was reached through a corridor lined with reproduction portraits of the same hero. I'd later learn that the world's galleries held over two hundred portraits of Napoleon's nemesis. This corridor had no fewer than forty reproductions on display. I recognised one by Goya but the rest, by such as Robert Home and Sir Thomas Lawrence, were unknown to me. It was daunting enough that the eyes of forty Wellingtons followed me down the corridor.

On entering the dining room, patrons were faced with a full-size reproduction of William Sadler's crowded vision of the actual battle. Hundreds of dead and dying sabre-swinging and bugle-blowing soldiers jostled within this startling three foot by six canvas. An armoury of crossed swords and muskets cluttered every other available wall space. It was as much a dining room as it was a memorial to a slaughter and neither sat comfortably with the other, particularly if you took your porterhouse rare.

With one ear to my neighbouring table and one eye to the battle scene on the wall, I barely noticed the quality of the meal nor of the wine that I must have consumed. I became aware of the waiter standing close to my shoulder. His intent was not to clear the plates. No, he was concentrating on the storyteller's narrative as closely as was I.

And what a story it was. We – the waiter and I – never learned the name of the heroic medical orderly because it was the storyteller himself. The entire saga was delivered in the first person as if it had been Semper who staunched the bleeding and stretchered the wounded from the battle field.

Rather than '…the orderly said…' it was '…I said…' There were no phrases like '…the young orderly dashed to the surgeon's side…' but rather '…I dashed to the surgeon's side…' Allman Semper, a man of some forty years, was, impossibly, the fifteen-year-old medical orderly tending to the battlefield wounded some sixty years earlier.

I confess to having risked an occasional thruppence to watch side-show performers professing to be the resurrected souls of historic notables such as George Washington or Julius Caesar. Most of them are so laughably unconvincing as not to be worth the entrance fee but I've admired those few who have pursued a bit of research and tried to affect a voice from the past. But Allman Semper told his story as one who had actually been at Waterloo, who knew everything that there was to know about Waterloo. He knew the names of the wounded, he knew the names of the surgeons and he could describe the tools of their grisly trade as if he handled them every day. Semper could describe, in daily detail, his London childhood, his limited schooling, his enlistment and the training undertaken in becoming a medical orderly. He knew as much anatomy as was known to an orderly in 1815 and he could list the daily rations of the troopers. The uniforms and insignia of every division and battalion in both armies were known to him, as was the bore of every pistol, musket and cannon.

We, the well-to-do couple, the waiter and myself, were transfixed as Semper recounted the horrors and the heroisms of Waterloo. We fled with him when the hospital tent came under attack and silently cheered as he pulled an officer from beneath his dying horse. We felt the warm stickiness of a soldier's blood as he dressed a sword wound. We heard the cannon, the screams and, finally, his rasping cheer when it was over.

And then the waiter, who had absentmindedly sat at an adjoining table during Wellington's final charge, remembered where he was and started clearing away the vestiges of my meal. I sat back, exhausted, and studied Sadler's huge battle scene hanging on the opposite wall. Searching for a young medical orderly.

The well-to-do couple rose and shook hands with Semper before departing. I caught up with him just before he mounted the stairs that would take him to his room. I introduced myself, we shook hands and I offered to buy him a nightcap in the saloon bar.

He was taller than I'd thought and good-looking in a weathered sort of way. His tanned and lined face was dominated by deep-set and dark green eyes and I found his permanent, lopsided grin to be off-putting – cynical – as if he held everything and everyone around him in mildly amusing contempt.

'Thank you, young sir,' he grinned. And then, when we were settled in leather armchairs with brandies to hand, he continued, 'You were eavesdropping on my rigmarole...you and that waiter.'

I nodded. 'Hard not to. It's an amazing story. But...'

His grin widened as he held up a silencing hand. He'd answered this question many times before. 'How could I have been at Waterloo? I'd have to be...what? Seventy-two-years old?' He swirled his brandy snifter, put it to his nose and then took the smallest of sips. 'It's all a load of falsehoods, old chap…all fiction.'

'But –'

Again he interrupted. 'It's all in the telling…and in the research. There's not a lot about Waterloo and Wellington that I don't know. I've spent hours in libraries.'

I too took a sip of brandy. It was, appropriately, Napoleon. 'But it sounded so real…so convincing.'

He bowed shallowly from his seat. 'Thank you. I take that as a compliment. The trick is to tell it as if I was there…in the first person. It's theatre…scripted. I spend as much time memorising the script as I do researching it.'

'Damn good script,' I mused. 'And superbly delivered. You had me in.' Another sip. 'I completely overlooked the impossibility of you being at Waterloo.'

Allman saluted me with his snifter and grinned. There was nothing cynical in this grin – he was genuinely pleased and he looked all the better for it. 'I thank you again, old chap. All performers wallow in compliments, and that's what I am – an actor, an entertainer. Some people sing, some play an instrument. I tell stories and people pay me to hear them.'

'And the people to whom you were telling it?'

'Last night was the Havershams. This evening it was the Crowleys.'

'Friends of yours?'

'Hardly, old chap. They're clients. They pay me to entertainment them.'

'An audience of two?'

'Exactly. Storytelling is the oldest of performing arts. It pre-dates writing by centuries. Time was when a culture's laws, its history and suchlike were passed on through word of mouth. If the narrator makes it entertaining and more theatrical, then the stories become easier to remember. Bards and minstrels are part of the tradition.'

He drained his snifter, took a notebook from his jacket pocket and consulted it. 'Tomorrow evening I'll be dining with the Paulsons. It'll be the same story again, I'm afraid, so perhaps you should bring something to read as you dine.'

He snorted a brief laugh as he stood and held out his hand. 'At least that damn waiter can concentrate on his tasks rather than eavesdropping with his mouth open. He's heard that story through at least five previous tellings. Thanks for the drink, old chap.'

And he was gone. I mulled over Allman Semper's brief historical lecture for a further ten minutes before I too climbed the stairs to my room.

*

His audience on the following evening was much older. Old enough, surely, to have been chipper when Waterloo actually took place. Old enough to have been contemporaries of the fictitious young medical orderly.

Mrs Paulson was a tiny woman made larger by mauve crinoline regalia that might have been fashionable in the Duke of Wellington's circles. She had the complexion of a dried apple but her eyes were bright and inquisitive.

Her husband might once have towered over her but a pronounced stoop rendered him only a little taller. He was as thin as a bean and relied heavily on two canes. His suit also belonged to an earlier fashion and had obviously been tailored to a sturdier physique. It took him an age to manoeuvre across the dining room and he seemed quite frustrated with himself. His eyes, like his wife's, revealed a sparkling intellect amplifying, I assumed, the frustration with his failing constitution.

Allman Semper was the perfect gentleman; easing his clients into their chairs and guiding them through the complications of wine lists and menus which, I might add, were each adorned with yet more portraits of the duke and more illustrations of assorted military hardware.

Semper's suggestion that I should bring something to read between courses had prompted me to gather a clutch of brochures from the agricultural show. Inspired by his in-depth research, I had determined to follow suit. To learn all that there was to know of those enterprises which might join Ralph Gordon's riverboat exposition – the key to my aspirational novel. Presumptuous it might be, but I'd sensed a bit of kinship with Semper, the professional storyteller. I'd even fancied that his fictional young medical orderly and my fictional Ralph Gordon might have become friends.

So, as Allman's elderly clients chewed their way through the adventures of his young orderly, I chewed my way through the mechanics of hay-cutters, the chemical composition of sheep dip and the intricacies of pedal-powered scroll saws.

I don't know whether he'd abbreviated his story or whether the Paulsons' bedtime encroached, but the trio took their leave of the dining room quite a bit earlier than had Allman's previous clients. As the waiter escorted the doddering couple from their table, the storyteller sat at mine, bringing with him the best part of an opened bottle of burgundy.

Having poured two generous glasses, he began flipping through my brochures. 'This your line of business, old chap? Agricultural hardware?'

I'd not noticed, during our previous brief conversation, how much his storytelling voice differed from his conversational voice. The former was brisk and conspiratorial. His tone now was drawled – languid.

I briefly described my business at the agricultural show and then went on to explain, not without some trepidation, my ambition to write a novel and the reason for my collection of brochures.

'Wonderful. Do you have a synopsis? Characters?'

I started to outline the plot and it came as a bit of a surprise to find that I did, in fact, have a rough synopsis, and a central character and even a picturesque setting.

Allman topped up our glasses and signalled for another bottle. 'Sounds excellent, old chap. Slip in a spot of romantic interest and you'll have a full count.'

'Thanks,' I said, uncertain how I'd slip any romantic interest into my story. I reckoned on Ralph Gordon being too busy with heroic deeds and becoming wealthy to worry about romance. But the image of young Ralph steering his riverboat with one arm wrapped around the waist of a beautiful woman – a woman that he'd rescued from the clutches of a villain – was tantalising. I filed the image away.

'Can I ask you about your storytelling? How you started? It's a rather unusual pursuit.'

'Of course, old man.' He took a decent sip of the burgundy, placed his glass on the table and then leaned back to stare at the ceiling. 'I'm a convict…'

I gasped. He lifted a calming hand. 'True. I'm a convict…was a convict. I was aboard the *Hougoumont*. You've no doubt heard of it. The last convict transport to arrive in Perth four years ago.'

'But what had you done? What was your crime?'

'Ahhh…guilt by association, old man. Association with the Fenians.'

Naturally, I knew of the Fenians. Knew that they were sometimes called the Irish Republican Brotherhood and that they were a bunch of separatist radicals. I knew that they'd sometimes resorted to violent protests and that there had been a notorious escape from Hobart some twenty years earlier. I'd been but a lad so I didn't remember the details – probably never knew them – but I recalled that some people thought the escapee a rogue and others thought him a hero. His name was – what? John Mitchell? Not sure. I thought his alias was Mister Wright.

'But surely you're not a –' I began.

'Irish?' He cut me off. 'For heaven's sake, old man. Do I sound like an Irishman?'

'Well, no…'

'Let me tell the story. I worked for *The London News*. I was assigned to an aged journalist to run his stories back to the office when he was too busy, or too drunk, to do it himself. The man, Grantham, was an absolute sot but also related to the editor by way of a distant marriage.' He sipped his burgundy and gave a wry smile which did nothing to diminish his cynical countenance. 'Mind you, I use the term journalist advisedly. Grantham's writings were dreary. When he was too drunk to write anything that made sense, I'd rewrite his scribble and add a few evocative lines of my own.'

'Evocative?'

'Little anecdotes about the propensities…the intimacies of the characters. An example: we were sent to attend a meeting of the Republican Brotherhood – the Fenians.' He waved a dismissive hand although I'd not interrupted him. 'Not the militaristic Fenians that one reads about. These were, in the main, priests and grandmothers and political hopefuls and suchlike. Peaceful folk…arbitrators rather than combatants. They were, in a word, tiresome. The meeting was tiresome, the speakers were tiresome and the account that my drunken superior had me run back to the office was as tiresome as was he himself.'

'And you…'

'I took his tedious drivel and inserted some evocative recitations.'

'I'm still uncertain about what you call evocative.'

'The opposite of tiresome, old man. In this instance, I inserted several creative phrases.'

'For example?'

He paused for more burgundy, leaned back in his chair and seemed to take an extraordinary interest in a pair of crossed sabres hanging above the doorway. Eventually, he settled on an example that pleased him. 'One of the speakers was a doddering old priest who rattled on about Irish lore. I sat on a rear pew alongside an old chap who was near to dozing off. "You've heard this before?" I enquired. He stirred from his torpor, listened for a moment and opined, "This is all the old dodderer ever spouts on about."'

'Sounds rather –'

'Uninspirational,' completed Allman. 'So I wrote "Ardent nationalist, Father Gallagher, kindled his audience with evocative accounts of Ireland's violent past."'

'Stretching the truth a bit,' I suggested.

Allman nodded, 'Unashamedly, old chap. No apologies. The next speaker was an old woman who'd lost a son in some sort of skirmish. Nothing political, just a pub fight. Her ramble was about peace and forgiveness. I prompted the old chap on the bench and he responded with something along the lines of "Silly old Biddy thinks we should all turn the other cheek and hug one another."'

'Which you interpreted as?'

'"Audience rejected cry for calm and clemency from a victim's mother."'

'Clever,' I conceded. 'But untrue, surely?'

'No…not entirely untrue.' He drained his glass and stood up so suddenly that I felt momentarily threatened by his tall frame looming over me. But then he thrust out a hand and drawled, 'I've no clients tomorrow evening, old chap. Perhaps we could dine together?'

'Er…yes,' I rose to shake his hand. 'Yes…certainly. I look forward to it.'

*

It being the final day of the agricultural show, most vendors began dismantling their displays and booths just after midday. Mine, being a simpler display, took me but two hours to pack my fencing tools and samples of wire and suchlike into the Throsby Fencing Supply Co. dray. My order books went into an oilskin satchel under the seat.

I was back at the Hero of Waterloo Hotel by mid-afternoon, where, by chance, I encountered Allman Semper as he was descending the broad staircase.

'Hello there.' He made quite a theatre of withdrawing a pocket watch from his waistcoat and consulting it. An unnecessary gesture as he would surely be aware of the time. 'What's this? Three o'clock? Have you sold all of your wares or have you deserted your post?'

I chuckled, as I was meant to do. 'Neither. The show concluded today. I packed up earlier than usual.'

'Ah. So will we still be dining this evening?'

'Oh, yes. I'm allowed two extra days to recuperate before reporting back to Mr Throsby.'

'Excellent. Then perhaps we might meet a little earlier in the saloon for pre-dinner drinks?' He flipped open his watch again. 'Shall we say six o'clock…in three hours from now?'

'I look forward to it,' I said as we passed each other. I upwards to my room. He downwards to where I did not ask.

*

Allman was wreathed in blue smoke when I arrived. He waved his cigar towards an empty chair on the opposite side of a low table. His morning coat was draped over the arm of an adjacent chair – close to hand against the arrival of other patrons.

'Have a seat, young fellow.' He edged an elegant crystal wine glass across the table. 'Madeira satisfactory?'

I'm not particularly fond of sweet fortified wines. Ale or burgundy were my preferences. I noticed that Semper had a near-full decanter of the sticky liqueur in front of him, so I deferred to his offering. In truth, my eagerness to learn more of his arrest and transportation overruled my dislike for his choice of tipple.

'Thank you, Allman. That would be excellent.' I took a reluctant sip. 'You were telling me about your involvement with the Fenians.'

'Never involved, young fellow. Falsely accused…of being a sympathiser.'

'How could that be?'

He placed his glass back on the table and rested his elbows on each arm of his chair. Then he steepled his fingers under his chin and pondered for just a moment before speaking. 'I hadn't realised that my evocative jottings had come to the attention of the police, who, typically, misinterpreted them as being seditious. One detective in particular took it upon himself to take issue. His name was Massey and, apparently, he'd been injured in a Fenian street battle.'

'So this Massey had a grudge?'

'Oh, yes. And it was unfortunately coincidental that London had suffered a resurgence of bombings and bashings by the Brotherhood. Massey had been in the centre of several violent incidents. Oh, yes… He'd a grudge against everything Fenian and everyone connected, no matter how tenuously, to anything Irish.'

Just then a small group entered the salon, two gentlemen and three ladies, one of whom seemed considerably older that the others. I took them to be two married couples and someone's mother or, alternatively, someone's mother-in-law. They were engaged in animated conversation and didn't notice Allman discreetly slipping back into his morning coat. Obviously my companion had a care for how he presented to others. Equally obvious was that he didn't care how he'd presented to me.

The chatty group took seats as far from us as was possible. Even so, Allman lowered his voice to continue his tale.

'That couple,' he nodded towards the new arrivals, 'she in the russet gown. Clients of mine. I gave them my story of Cortez last month.'

'Cortez? The Portuguese explorer? The –'

'Spanish, old chap. Not Portuguese. Hernàn Cortez. He who slaughtered the Aztecs and claimed Mexico.'

'But what of the young orderly at Waterloo?'

'My current persona. I was a soldier with Cortez. Marched on Tenochtitlan in 1519.' He frowned and placed a recalling finger on his forehead. 'Mid-August if I remember correctly.'

'But…?'

"Different story each month, old chap. Last month it was Cortez and before that a studio apprentice to Francisco Goya. Dark times they were. What with Napoleon invading and suchlike.'

He replenished his glass from the decanter and offered it to me. I added a drop or two to my own glass, not because I needed any more of the syrupy stuff but because it gave me a moment to digest what I'd just heard.

'A different story. A different persona each month?'

'And each month my regular clients have me dine with them and entertain them as the new persona.' He smiled his cynical smile. 'And pay me quite adequately.'

'Extraordinary. Can I ask who you'll be next month?'

'I'm considering one or two possibilities, old chap. I'm still researching and refining the stories. Making them more believable and trying them out before I decide. There's no hurry. I still have several regular clients who haven't been to Waterloo yet.'

'I'd not fully appreciated that this is your occupation – telling stories. You don't have any other…business…trade?'

'No need. As I've explained. Storytelling is an age-old and honourable pursuit. Between you and me, old chap, I do rather nicely. Fifteen shillings from each of twenty clients each month. Added, of course, to a damn fine dinner paid for by the clients every time I entertain them.' Another sip of Madeira. 'Many times more lucrative than if I were to tell the story from a theatre's stage.'

I determined to calculate his income after dinner and when I'd retired to my room. Then I was distracted by the thought of dinner. 'Perhaps we should go to the dining room,' I suggested.

We both opted for the roasted mutton with mint sauce, which proved to be a wise choice, whereas the figgy dowdy with lumpy custard was not. Strangely, the chef seemed to have an Achilles heel when it came to custard. Nevertheless, we were quite replete as we lingered over port and I prompted Allman to continue.

'I was nabbed during a street march,' he began. 'A peaceful enough affair. Just a few lukewarm hotheads with banners and suchlike. I was to follow the march in anticipation of a police confrontation.'

'Detective Massey?'

'Correct. Massey and fifty of his ilk. No warning whatsoever.' He leaned forward, elbows on the table, as if he was wary of being overheard. 'I regained consciousness in a cell with twenty others. I later learned that Massey had fixed me as a target and laid me out with a truncheon blow from behind.'

'But you were only an observer. And…and…you're not Irish.'

'Nor the only Englishman to be incarcerated. There were two others…known informers. Massey separated we three from the rest and grouped us together on the same conspiracy charge.'

'But didn't your newspaper have lawyers?'

'Yes, and they threw me to the wolves.'

'What? How?'

'You'll remember that I told you that my debauched master, Grantham, was hand in glove with the editor? Apparently he had taken issue with my interference with his writings. He fabricated a catalogue of untruths about me. Convinced the editor and the lawyers that I'd brought disgrace to the newspaper. I was dismissed even as I sat in that cell with the two real criminals. Dismissed without recourse to argument. Denied legal representation.'

I was flabbergasted. True, tales of injustice were not uncommon, but hearing of such inequitable treatment first hand was astounding.

Semper gave his lopsided grin at my loss for words. 'I've documented every word of the court proceedings. I'd plenty of time aboard the *Hougoumont* during the passage to Freemantle. Precisely eighty-nine days. For a convict ship, it wasn't as bad as it might have been. She carried two hundred convicts. Sixty of us were non-violent political prisoners. We were kept apart, given privileges, no shackles, extended deck time and suchlike. Even writing materials.'

'That was…what? Three years ago? How long was your sentence? How is it that you're here in Sydney?' A thought rang in my head. 'Are you an escapee?'

Allman chuckled. 'Nothing so romantic, old chap. Apparently the English had broken an agreement by sending us to Fremantle. We were given tickets of -leave after six months.'

I sat back, staring at Sadler's painting without seeing it. 'Astonishing,' I ventured. 'This story could rival your Cortez and Waterloo inventions.'

'Possibly,' he nodded. 'Possibly.'

I was about to say more but he stood up abruptly and, again, I was taken aback by his looming posture. He thrust out his hand. 'Well met, old chap. I've business to attend to tomorrow so we probably won't meet again. I wish you well with your hardware and your novel.'

He left me to pay the bill.

*

I was, for the last time, dining alone. As the waiter placed my dish of grilled fish before me, he enquired, 'I couldn't help but overhear a little of your companion's story last evening, sir. What did you think?'

'Outrageous.' I answered heatedly. 'One of the worst cases of conspiracy and injustice I have ever heard.'

'Ah. He'll be pleased to hear that, sir.'

His comment took a moment to penetrate my outrage. 'Pleased? Why would he be pleased to hear it?'

'I thought you realised, sir. You're the first person to have spoken with his latest persona.'